WAS THIS THE END OF …

"Keep looki… …ople don't just di…

"Why not?" … "All those houses …

Eyes narrowing, Remo grabbed Captain Holden by the throat with both fists. He lifted him off his feet for emphasis. "Get your men together. You find my friend. Or they'll be looking for your pieces next."

They found the Master of Sinanju among the corn. Chiun's head was turned so one cheek rested in the dirt. A solitary fly crawled out from behind Chiun's shell of an ear. Angrily, Remo killed it with a violent snap of his fingers.

Remo lay a finger against the Master's carotid artery. He felt nothing. His stomach sank. He stifled a sob. . . .

The '90s had turned into a nightmare for the Destroyer—and the nightmare had only just begun.

#84

The Destroyer

GROUND ZERO

WARREN MURPHY & RICHARD SAPIR

A SIGNET BOOK

SIGNET
Published by the Penguin Group
Penguin Books USA Inc., 375 Hudson Street,
New York, New York 10014, U.S.A.
Penguin Books Ltd, 27 Wrights Lane,
London W8 5TZ, England
Penguin Books Australia Ltd, Ringwood,
Victoria, Australia
Penguin Books Canada Ltd, 2801 John Street,
Markham, Ontario, Canada L3R 1B4
Penguin Books (N.Z.) Ltd, 182-190 Wairau Road,
Auckland 10, New Zealand

Penguin Books Ltd, Registered Offices:
Harmondsworth, Middlesex, England

First published by Signet, an imprint of New American Library, a division of Penguin Books USA Inc.

First Printing, April 1991
10 9 8 7 6 5 4 3 2 1

Printed in the United States of America

PUBLISHER'S NOTE
This is a work of fiction. Names, characters, places, and incidents either are the product of the author's imagination or are used fictitiously, and any resemblance to actual persons, living or dead, events, or locales is entirely coincidental.

For Bill Berry, Korac MacArthur, and all who write to P.O. Box 2505, Quincy, MA 02269—AKA the Glorious House of Sinanju—seeking wisdom.

The box is empty.

1

La Plomo, Missouri, was dying.

For almost fifty years it had been dying. A farm town nestled in the rolling paradise of Adair County, La Plomo had been hit hard by the Depression, although it had never been a dust-bowl town. Back then the Santa Fe Railroad stopped at La Plomo a dozen times each day, hauling La Plomo corn, wheat, and soybeans to market.

After the war, La Plomo started to change. The ugly blacktop highways went up. The trains came less frequently. To the north, beyond Grizzy Creek, nearby Kirkland flowered into a center of commerce, but La Plomo remained a modest farm town. It boasted only one business strip, consisting of a drugstore, restaurant, and general store across the street from a simple rectangle of grass on which sat a cabled-down Korean War-vintage jet fighter that had been placed there for children to play on. Such was La Plomo's modest town square.

This incongruously modern touch did nothing to change the basic character of La Plomo life. Fathers still hunted squirrels with their male children. Skinny-dipping in the watering hole was a summer tradition. Square-dancing often led to marriage.

Adult La Plomons entertained themselves with

their outdoor bean festivals, where locals repeated the same cornball gags their great-grandfathers had yarned a century ago. Only the names of the local politicians changed.

A pocket of changelessness in a fast-moving world was La Plomo. Always a close-knit community, the farms kept it that way, all through the long cycle of seasons, good and bad, to the present day.

Then came the drought. The wheat dried up. Even the tall green corn withered and shriveled. The economy started to dry up too. Foreclosures began. Farms that had been in families since the Civil War were sold off to strangers. People pulled up their roots and moved to the city and its civilized horrors. More than a community was being tested. A way of life began to break apart.

La Plomo truly started to die then.

On the night La Plomo, Missouri, gasped its last—literally—Aldace Noiles lay in bed contemplating the changes he had seen in his life. It had sprinkled some that evening. A few final drops pattered on the eaves of Noiles's simple house. He enjoyed lying alone in bed, in the dark, the sound of rain sprinkling his roof. It made him feel safe and warm, which to a sixty-seven-year-old widower was a not-unimportant thing.

Aldace had been La Plomo's postmaster during the postwar years. He had been but a lowly mail clerk when his draft number had been called back in 1943. When he returned in '46, the postmaster announced his retirement and Aldace slid right into his old job. La Plomo was that small. The population then was less than two thousand. Tonight, Aldace reflected, it was considerably less than a thousand.

He had no inkling of it, but by the time the dawning sun burned off the strangely yellow prairie mists, the total population of La Plomo would drop to zero.

It was the events of the 1943–46 period of his life that made Aldace Noiles appreciate the simple pleasure of lying awake in bed without worry or fear. Sure, La Plomo was hurting. But it would go on, might even prosper again one day. Aldace Noiles might not see that fine day, but he knew it would come.

Aldace Noiles appreciated being alive. He had been with the Rangers in Burma, where the Japanese were dug in deep. After months of fearsome fighting, the Japs had retreated into caves and the only way to get them out was to burn them out.

Ranger Aldace Noiles had wielded a flamethrower, and the things he had to do with that terrible tool, the power fire had over human flesh, haunted his sleep for years and years after he had returned home.

Aldace had a simple prayer in those days. It was: "Please, dear Lord, let me die in my own bed."

He mumbled it for the first time in a rain–swollen foxhole. It stayed with him during the long voyage home on a troop ship. Even after he had returned to his simple bed, physically whole but emotionally impressed by war, Aldace made a special point of kneeling at bedtime and repeating his midnight mantra. War made a man appreciate his simple joys like nothing else.

These days, Aldace Noiles invoked that prayer less religiously than he once had. He was retired now. Didn't even drive anymore. Dying in bed looked more and more like a sure thing. But every so often—say, once or twice a month—he remembered to say it.

Tonight happened to be one of those nights.

Aldace Noiles wasn't sure when he fell asleep.

At his age, sleep was a stealthy fog that stole up on a body slowly.

He woke up suddenly, in surprise. He seldom awoke at night anymore. No worries troubled his rest. He had a government pension. The mortage was paid off back in '66. But on this last night, the night he was destined to die in bed along with the remaining 862 inhabitants of La Plomo, Missouri, Aldace Noiles shot bolt upright, clutching at his throat.

It was the stinging, coughing sensation that he noticed first. There was a burning tang smelling faintly of geraniums in his dry old nostrils. Like a beached trout, Aldace took a gulp of air through his mouth. He released it like a dog spitting out a throat-caught bone. Except the bone wouldn't expel.

Aldace noticed the yellowish haze in the room. Moonlight coming through the gauze curtains made the haze shine evilly.

Aldace coughed again. This time a glob of reddish phlegm spattered on the bedspread.

Aldace looked at it in horror. His first thought was that he had cancer. But cancer didn't come on sudden-like to rob the breath. And Aldace had smoked his last Marlboro back in '59.

The coughing racked Noiles's pigeon-chested torso. He fell out of bed, faded pajama legs flapping against his thin shins as he stumbled, coughing, to the green-tiled bathroom.

He ran water into a drinking glass and gulped it down.

The water came up as a pinkish vomit. It had no sooner hit his stomach than it regurgitated again, along with the creamed beef and garden-fresh peapods that had been his dinner.

The coughing got worse. His lungs labored for air, but each breath was shallower, each exhalation more painful. He spat another bloody clot of viscous matter, and feeling himself about to retch again, hung his head over the porcelain toilet.

Then he heard the sounds. They came through the walls. Coughing. Other people coughing. Choruses of coughing, racking, crying. Someone screamed. It sounded like old Widow Story.

Somehow Aldace Noiles found the strength to stumble out his front door. The grass was damp under his bare feet. The night was cool, but the air was not. It burned his lungs. He thought the grass burned his feet too.

Looking up and down the street, Aldace saw lights in the houses come on. One here, another there. La Plomo was awakening. And Aldace could see why. The moth-bedeviled auras of the streetlights were yellow and hazy. They were cool blue lights, not the harsh halogen lamps that Mayor Dent had tried to force on them. They shouldn't be yellow. The pure night air of La Plomo should not be yellow.

A car started up and screeched back out of its driveway. He recognized young Randal Bloss at the wheel. The car careened down the street and went up on a lawn, crushing a mailbox perched on a whitewashed post. Bloss stumbled out, holding his throat, his tongue out, coughing and hacking. He ran around in an aimless circle, like a beheaded chicken, and then simply lay down on his back, looking up at the hazy yellow air and coughing out his life.

"I'll get help, Randal," Aldace hollered. He returned to his living room. The phone in his ear was silent. No dial tone. He plunged back out to the street.

"Don't you fret!" he called. But Randal Bloss' struggles were growing feeble. His forearms folded, the hands hanging from his wrists flaccidly. He reminded Aldace of a beetle on its back after being hit by a squirt of Black Flag.

Aldace plunged down the street. The air was worse here. He stumbled twice. His own coughing worsened and the cold sweats started. But he fought on, determined to make it to the nearby town square.

The air was worse there. Not merely harder to breathe, but more yellow. Frighteningly yellow. And Aldace saw why.

The Sabrejet, which had been placed there in 1965 after the town fathers had exhausted every effort to have a steam engine—a more fitting symbol of La Plomo's former glory—placed in the square, was expelling something from its tailpipe. It came out in furious yellowish streams.

The truth dawned on Aldace Noiles then. His mind had refused to accept it. Until now.

"My God, it's gas!" Aldace croaked. "Poison gas!"

And all over town, the hack-cough symphony swelled to a crescendo.

Aldace Noiles knew then there would be no escape, and so he stumbled back toward home and the comfort of his lonely bed. He didn't make it. Aldace collapsed on the burning green grass, coughing up crimson clots, his body racked with the shakes.

Aldace Noiles was not going to die in bed after all—not in the peaceful manner he had been counting on.

But at the last, Aldace was a simple God-fearing man. He would accept what the Good Lord had in store for him without complaint. If only it didn't hurt so deep.

As he died, he coughed out a little prayer. Not

for himself, but for the good people of La Plomo. Especially the young ones, who hadn't had much of a future when the day began, but now had absolutely none at all.

Their pitiful cries scorched his ears.

His last act was to stick his shaking fingers in his ears to block out the Godawful din. Even that did not help.

Later, the morticians had to break his stiff arms the better to fit him in his coffin. By that time, La Plomo was a silent necropolis in which no songbirds sang and the drone of insects was curiously absent.

2

His name was Remo and he was being ignored.

The ignoring began in North Korea, in the village of Sinanju, to be exact. Sinanju was not much of a village as villages go. It was basically an apron of mud flats overlooking a barren gray sea, the West Korea Bay. Back of the mud flats the huts clustered, ramshackle, weathered, and unfit for human habitation.

It was nevertheless one of the best places to live out your days north of the thirty-eighth parallel. No men from Sinanju were ever drafted into the People's Army. No taxes were ever collected, not since the year 1945, when an emissary of the new communist government arrived to insist that the village must now pay its taxes, even though taxes had been waived in the long-ago days when Korea was ruled by the Dragon Throne.

The tax collector—whose name is not recorded in the annals of Sinanju—was handed his head. Literally.

He had stood there facing the Master of Sinanju, whom he assumed was something akin to a mayor or village chief, repeating his request to the Master, because the old man was apparently deaf. He kept saying, "What?" in a querulous voice.

"If you dispute the amount of the tax," the tax collector had explained, "you may file for an abatement."

"I do not know that word," said the Master of Sinanju, suddenly hearing very well. "It sounds Western." He spat.

"An abatement is the return of unfair tax."

"I declare all taxes on Sinanju unfair. You may go now."

"I must insist."

Finally the Master of Sinanju, who was called Chiun, made a vague gesture with his impossibly long fingernails. The tax collector remembered the gesture to his dying instant.

The tax collector heard the one called Chiun say, "Put out both hands."

Thinking that he had prevailed upon the old man, the tax collector obeyed. His neatly severed head fell into his upraised palms.

His ears echoed to the Master of Sinanju's bitter, "There is your abatement." But he heard the words not. He was dead.

"Thus did Kim Il-Sung, first leader of communist North Korea, learn of the House of Sinanju's attitude toward his mastery of the land," Chiun said gravely, many years later, a wise finger lifted to the sky. "By being ignored."

Remo Williams heard this story sitting around the village square with the very same Master of Sinanju. Chiun's wizened old face broke into radiating wrinkles of joy as he finished his tale. He slapped one silken knee. The light in his eyes was as clear as agates polished by a meandering stream. His thin frame and wispy beard shook with humor. Even the puffs of hair over each ear seemed to vibrate with mirth.

Remo laughed. The villagers laughed, a little nervously, because they were outnumbered three to one by Mongol warriors, guests of the Master of Sinanju. The Mongols roared. Their laughter shook the very blue in the sky. Back from the shore, at the inner edge of the village, scores of Mongol ponies whinnied and dropped dung. The sound of dropping dung was like a noisome intermittent rain.

This had gone on all month, since they had journeyed on horseback from distant China, bearing the treasure of Genghis Khan.

"Pretty good story, Little Father," Remo Williams, the only white man in the gathering, said.

He was ignored.

The significance of this was lost on him until, hours later, with the sun sinking and the moon turning into a crystal bowl low in the cobalt sky, the Mongol leaders—Boldbator, who called himself Khan, and the bandit chief Kula—drew themselves up and offered farewell toasts to the dying blue of the sky.

The Master of Sinanju bade farewell to the Mongols with Oriental gravity. Ornate snuff bottles were exchanged. The bowing went on for nearly an hour.

Remo placed his hands on Kula's shoulders and Kula returned the gesture. He and Boldbator also exchanged the traditional Mongol gesture of farewell. Warm words were exchanged. They perfumed the air as the entire village trailed the Mongols to their houses.

"Farewell, brave brothers of the horse," Chiun, Reigning Master of Sinanju, called after them. "Sinanju owes you a great debt."

"It is good to know that the ties which bound Lord Genghis to Sinanju survive in the modern world," thundered Boldbator.

"Have a good one, guys," Remo called. Everyone looked at Remo, unsure how to respond to the white man's empty words.

Remo grinned sheepishly.

Then the Mongols mounted and arrayed their ponies, Boldbator and Kula taking the lead. Kula raised the nine-horsetail standard of Genghis Khan high in a one-handed salute. Arnold Schwarzenegger and Sylvester Stallone together would have needed all four hands to hold it off the ground. But Kula lifted it with no especial effort.

"Farewell, comrades," they sang, starting off.

Remo and Chiun watched the undulating rumps of the ponies disappear into the gathering dusk, dropping their seemingly ceaseless supply of malodorous fertilizer.

When they were no longer visible, the villagers let out a collective sigh of relief. The men almost wept with the joy of having supped with Mongol raiders and survived. The women stopped walking with their thighs together, no longer in fear of being ravished.

"Well, that's the last of them," Remo said.

"I thought they would never leave," Chiun spat, turning to go.

Walking carefully so as not to step in anything organic, Remo followed, saying, "Am I missing something? Didn't you just swear undying admiration to those guys?"

Again he was ignored.

Shrugging, Remo fell in behind the purposeful figure of the Master of Sinanju, who strode up to the one sound edifice in the entire village, the House of the Masters, built of rare woods back in the days of the pharaohs.

Chiun undid the intricate locks and pushed the door open. He disappeared within. Remo started to follow. The door slammed in his face. Remo stopped, put his hands on his hips.

"What did I do!" he complained loudly. Silence greeted his demand. He pounded on the door. "Chiun? Open up. You hear me?"

No answering sound came from the House of the Masters. Remo put one ear to the polished wood.

He heard an extended adenoidal goose honking that was unmistakable proof that the Master of Sinanju has fallen asleep.

Annoyed, Remo returned to the village, wondering in Korean, "Anybody have a clue what bit Chiun?"

The villagers, who had been so friendly before—many of them had looked to Remo for protection against the barbarian Mongols—turned away.

"Ah, screw it," Remo muttered, seeking a place to sleep for the night. There was no sense pressing the villagers. Every one of them had seen Chiun's public rebuff. And they blindly followed the lead of their Master, not caring about his reasons.

"You ingrates just wait until I'm head of the village," he warned aloud.

The expressions that comment created ranged from startled to panic-stricken. Remo was suddenly surrounded by offers, ranging from a place to sleep for the night, to the best leftovers from the feast, and more than one Korean maiden offered him her maidenhead—but only on the condition that this was not revealed to the Master of Sinanju, who, everyone knew, abhorred whites.

Remo accepted a place to sleep from the aged Korean named Pullyang, who acted as village caretaker when Chiun was away. He wasn't in the mood for leftovers or maidenhead. He had eaten too much fish at the feast.

Led by Pullyang, he walked to the modest hut,

his thick-wristed hands stuffed in the pockets of his gray chinos. In his black T-shirt he looked nothing like a man who was the sole heir to the House of Sinanju, a line of assassins that had shaped the fortunes of the ancient world. Although he weighed less than 160 pounds, his scuffed Italian loafers barely left a mark in the eternal mud of Sinanju.

"Sometimes I don't know why I put up with his crap," Remo told Pullyang. His face wore a grim expression like a skull. Dark eyes gleamed in their hollows above prominent cheekbones. His mouth was an angry slash.

"You do not appreciate his awesome magnificence," Pullyang said sagely.

"Well, take it from me, he's a lot less magnificent when you have to deal with him every dingdong day."

Pullyang left Remo in a room furnished with only a tatami mat, murmuring, "You will miss him when he has journeyed into the Great Void."

"Who are you kidding?" Remo snorted. "That old reprobate will probably outlive me. Good night, Pullyang."

Pullyang padded off in ghostly silence.

Remo had trouble sleeping. Chiun's snit was not the cause. Chiun had had inexplicable snits like this one since the day, almost twenty years before, when Remo Williams—then a young Newark ex-cop—had been introduced to the frail Korean.

Remo had just come off death row. The hard way. He had been strapped sweating to the electric chair and shocked into oblivion.

Folcroft Sanitarium had been the name of the hell he later regained consciousness in. He was not dead. He had not died. He had been erased. All his identity records had been expunged. A fresh headstone bore his name. An orphan, he had no relatives, so the memory of Remo Williams, a good, if dumb, cop who had been framed for killing a pusher, existed only in the fading memories of a small circle of friends and coworkers.

All this was explained to Remo Williams as he got used to the too-tight skin of his new plastic-surgery-created face by Dr. Harold W. Smith, the head of Folcroft and director of CURE, a secret government agency that had been set up to salvage America, which was then falling into anarchy.

Remo had been selected to be its savior. He would become the instrument of righteousness in a corrupt world. And Chiun, disciple of the Sinanju martial-arts tradition, would be the one to transform him into that instrument.

Remo expressed his profound gratitude at the second chance at life by attempting to shoot the Master of Sinanju with a .38 revolver.

Chiun had not been young then. He looked as if he would topple in a brisk wind. Yet he had sidestepped, dodged, and eluded the attack in ways Remo had never imagined.

All five bullets missed. And unlike the average foot patrolman, Remo had been a pretty good shot.

That was the first icy breath of the power of Sinanju that blew through Remo Williams' soul.

Reluctantly he submitted himself to the training. He learned first to breathe, then to kill, and most important, not to be killed. In those early days, he thought he was being turned into a kind of government enforcer, but as the years passed and he learned not only to duplicate Chiun's bullet-dodging but also to climb sheer walls with the silent ease of a spider and run faster than a car, Remo realized he was becoming something more. He was becoming part of the House of Sinanju, the greatest assassins in human history.

That had been long ago. Their relationship had been through many rocky periods since.

The smell of pine needles wafting through the cool air brought Remo back to other days, previous trips to Sinanju, the center of the universe to the Masters of Sinanju, of which Remo was the first white man to qualify.

He remembered the first time he had come here, wounded and afraid, to battle his rival, the renegade Master Nuihc. Years later, Remo returned for the Master's Trial, in which he fought warriors from other lands, including the Scandinavian warrior-woman, Jilda, who later bore him a daughter. More recently he and Chiun had returned because he thought the Master of Sinanju was dying. Chiun had not been dying, but during those dangerous, uncertain days Remo had met and fallen in love with a tender maid of Sinanju named Mah-Li. Although circumstances tore him from her, he had returned to marry Mah-Li. With tragic consequences.

The thought of Mah-Li brought Remo to his feet. He drew on his chinos and slipped barefoot out into the night. Like a pale ghost, he floated to the burial yard of Sinanju.

He stood over the grave of Mah-Li the Beast—so called by the villagers because of her Western-style beauty—killed by an old enemy, the pupil of long-dead Nuihc. Had it really been four years ago? Remo wondered. Time was flying. Remo's new life was flying. His other life seemed like a half-remembered dream now.

Remo reached up into a towering fir tree and plucked several needles. As he sprinkled them onto Mah-Li's grave, he found it hard to remember her face with clarity. They had known each other less than a year. He wondered how his life would have gone had they wedded. He wondered how his life was going. How much longer could he work for America? Could Chiun?

He stood there turning vague unsettling thoughts over in his mind. No answers came. Slipping back to Pullyang's hut, he tried to find sleep.

Remo slept fitfully, as if plagued by nightmares. But when he awoke with the dawn, he could not remember any of them. But a cold unease sat in his belly like dry ice.

Pullyang padded up, carrying an awkwardly long reed pipe in one gnarled claw, as Remo stepped out into the light.

"What's up, Pullyang?" Remo asked.

"The Master bids me to inform you that he travels to America this day," Pullyang said in his thin cracked voice.

"Already? Where is he?"

"Packing. And he requires that you do the same if you intend to accompany him to America."

Remo lifted an eyebrow. "Intend?"

"Those were his exact words," Pullyang said solemnly.

"Tell him I'm packed," Remo growled.

Remo pulled on a white T-shirt, and slipping his bare feet into his loafers, he checked his rear pocket for his toothbrush. This constituted his packing.

Remo found the Master of Sinanju sitting in the saddle of a fine Mongolian pony, wearing a dull gray traveling robe. His face was sere.

"We going now?" Remo asked, approaching.

Chiun patted his pony in studied silence.

"Be that way, then," Remo muttered. He mounted his own pony, which Pullyang had saddled for him.

The Master of Sinanju forked his pony around

and started up a dirt road. "Farewell, Pullyang," he intoned. "Keep my village safe in my absence."

Remo followed, calling back, "Catch you later, Pullyang."

The dirt road lifted among rocks and leveled off at the edge of three huge empty superhighways marked Sinanju 1, 2, and 3. Chiun selected Sinanju 2 and sent his pony clopping along it.

His face unhappy, Remo rode in his wake.

They rode all the way to the Pyongyang airport, where the communist officials cheerfully stabled their horses for them and so retained their heads. Memories were long in Pyongyang.

Relations between North Korea and the civilized world being what they were, Remo and Chiun had to fly to Beijing to obtain a flight back to the U.S.

The layover in Beijing reminded Remo of his last assignment, the rescue of a Chinese dissident student named Zhang Zingzong, who had left the safety of America with Chiun, seeking the treasure of Genghis Khan. They had found the treasure, but the student had lost his life in the quest. It was the first time in many years that a CURE assignment had ended so badly, although from Chiun's point of view that was irrelevant. He had ended up with most of the treasure.

"Smitty's gonna have a fit about that student when we report in," Remo said casually. "Although I guess he has some idea, since it's been almost two months since we reported in."

They were seated in an airport waiting room. At the sound of Remo's voice, Chiun had flounced around to present Remo with his small back.

"Two can play this game," Remo muttered, ignoring him in turn.

Remo was ignored all the way across the Pacific Ocean too. He was forced to sit by himself during the five-hour transcontinental leg. And the taxi ride from Kennedy Airport to their home in Rye, New York, was thick with interminable silence.

Finally, pushing open the door to his house, Remo relented.

"Do you want to call Smith or shall I?" he asked in a subdued voice.

Chiun said nothing, so Remo reached for the phone. Clapping the receiver to his ear, he started dialing Folcroft Sanitarium when he realized the dial tone in his ear should not be there.

"Hey!" Remo said. "This phone is working."

Chiun, bent over a steamer trunk in another room, declined to look up.

"The line was disconnected before we left, remember? Smith must have had it repaired. That means he's been here. Probably planting more listening devices," Remo added sourly.

Chiun did not react.

"Don't you care?"

This time the Master of Sinanju did reply.

He said, "No." His voice was chilly. Then he shut the door.

"This is ridiculous," Remo exploded, "even for you."

He slammed the receiver and sidled up to the closed door.

"You know," he called through the wood, "I'd suffer a lot more if I knew what I did or said to piss you off."

Silence. Then a squeaky voice said, "It is not what you did, but what you did *not* do."

"Any hints?" Remo said, brightening. At least he wasn't being ignored anymore.

No further sound came through the door.

"I asked if you wanted to clue me in," Remo repeated in a hopeful voice.

The protracted silence made it clear to Remo that he was being ignored once again.

Remo stood in the middle of the living room—only a big-screen television gave any clue to the room's purpose, for there was not a stick of furniture in it—debating whether to call Smith or drop in, when the phone rang.

Remo scooped it up. His "Hello?" was a bark.

"Remo? This is Smith."

"Nice timing," Remo said, leaning on one hand against a wall. "We just got in."

"Er, I've been calling every half-hour for weeks."

Remo felt tiny vibrations under his palm. Frowning, he drove two stiff fingers into the plaster and extracted a round black microphone.

"It wouldn't be because you've got sensors planted in this place to warn you when we got back?" he asked suspiciously.

The pause was lengthy enough to let Remo know that Smith was debating whether or not to lie.

"What makes you say that?" Smith said at last. His tone was lemony and sharp.

"Well, the phone's fixed. I know the mice didn't do it, because the cheese is untouched."

"A necessity which I attended to as your superior," Smith said quickly. "Now, please, Remo, we have important matters to discuss."

"Yeah, well, Zhang is dead," Remo said, pocketing the bug. "I did what I could, but he bought it."

"I know."

"What'd you do?" Remo asked acidly. "Bug Mongolia?"

"The U.S. has intelligence assets in Asia," Smith explained. "That is the past. I was alerted to your presence in Pyongyang and in Beijing. There was no secure way to contact you en route. That is why I've been calling hourly."

"You said half-hourly," Remo pointed out. "But let it pass. If you're not upset about Zhang, what's the problem?"

"We have lost the town of La Plomo, Missouri. It has been eradicated."

"How so?"

"Poison gas. Every man, woman, and child was killed in his sleep."

Remo's voice tightened. "Is that a lot of people?"

"Less than a thousand. It was a small farm town, but that is not important. The La Plomo gassing took place three weeks ago. An FBI investigation has turned up nothing—no leads, no suspects. We're stymied. Washington has asked me to put you and Chiun on it."

"There's a problem with that," Remo said wearily.

The lemons in Smith's voice gave a sudden juicy squeeze. "Yes?"

"Chiun and I aren't currently on speaking terms."

"What have you done to offend him this time?"

"I like how I'm automatically branded as the instigator," Remo said sourly. "As for why, you'll have to ask Chiun. All I've gotten since Korea is cold silence interspersed with the occasional game of charades."

"Ask Chiun to come to the phone," Smith ordered crisply.

"Gladly," Remo said. He went to Chiun's room and knocked once. "Chiun, Smitty needs to talk to you."

There was no response.

"And boy, is he ticked off about losing Zhang," Remo added warningly. "He says we're through. Both of us. Hope you haven't unpacked."

The door banged open like a mousetrap snapping. Face stricken, the Master of Sinanju shot across the room like a gray ghost. The receiver came up to his wizened face and his squeaky voice poured out a torrent of plaintive words.

"It was all Remo's fault, Emperor Smith," he said rapidly. "He was careless, but all is not lost, for we have recovered the treasure of Genghis Khan, the greatest in history. You should see it. Rubies, emeralds, gold, and jade beyond description—"

Chiun paused, cocking his bald yellow head.

"No, I do not intend to contribute it to the national debt. Are you mad!"

Folding his arms, Remo leaned against a doorjamb, listening. He grinned.

"I thought you would be pleased that we did not allow Zhang to fall into unscrupulous hands," Chiun went on testily. "He was really quite unimportant. America has many defective Chinese students. Almost all of them are such, in fact."

"Chinese student defectors," Remo called over helpfully.

Chiun turned away, placing one hand over his free ear to block out the unwanted intrusion. He listened intently.

"Yes, Emperor. This is a private matter. I will explain later. I have my reasons. Very well. For this urgent assignment I will suffer whatever communications with the ungrateful one that are necessary. We shall leave at once."

Chiun hung up. He turned to Remo. His tiny mouth parted, causing his straggly beard to wriggle.

Remo beat him to the draw by a full second.

"Leave at once!" Remo shouted. "We just got here!"

"Silence," Chiun said imperiously. "I have agreed to suffer your companionship until this assignment is completed. But I will not be drawn into petty arguments. Remember this. Now you must pack."

"Pack? I haven't *un*packed!"

"Then let us hasten to the airport without delay."

The Master of Sinanju floated to the front door.

Remo hesitated. Frowning, he followed Chiun out to the car, grumbling, "All right, all right. But you could at least tell me who we're supposed to be this time out."

"I will be the unsurpassed Master of Sinanju," Chiun said haughtily, standing by the car door so that Remo could open it for him. "And you shall be what you always are—an insensitive clod."

"In that case," Remo said, stepping around to the driver's side, "open your own freaking door."

3

La Plomo, Missouri, was under siege.

Three weeks after the last of the stiff-limbed dead had been carted away, a crowd was gathered around the barbed-wire perimeter posted with "Keep Out" signs, where Missouri National Guardsmen stood guard wearing butyl rubber chemical-warfare garb and overboots, their heads enveloped in glassy-eyed gas masks.

The lawyers came first. The initial wave arrived a solid hour before the first weeping, bereaved relatives of the deceased. The anguished relatives had chased off the lawyers. The lawyers had retreated and returned with reinforcements.

Now, weeks later, the lawyers outnumbered the relatives, most of whom had quietly buried their dead and returned to their own lives.

The representatives of the media had dwindled down to single digits. Those that were left were trying to find someone who hadn't been asked the question "How does it feel to know that your blood relatives died in excruciating agony from improperly stored poison gas?" That no one had as yet had determined that an improperly stored nerve agent had had anything to do with the La Plomo disaster seemed not to faze them in the slightest.

When they couldn't extract an appropriate supporting sound bite from a distraught visitor or a stiff-necked National Guard sentry—who were completely unintelligible behind their gas masks anyway—the TV representatives simply sought out a handy spokesman from one of the many protest groups that had clustered around La Plomo with the same voraciousness as the big bluebottle flies buzzing the trampled-down cornfield at the north edge of the wire.

Remo tasted the smell of death hovering around the town of La Plomo before he saw the town itself. The airborne particles were probably less than one part per million, but his highly acute sense of smell detected the vaguely unappetizing stench as he coasted along U.S. 63 in his rented car.

"I think we're getting close," Remo called over his shoulder. "I'm gonna roll up the windows."

In the back seat, where he would not have to suffer a too-close proximity to his ungrateful pupil, the Master of Sinanju said, "You are too late by a mile. A country mile," he added.

Remo rolled up the windows anyway. He could endure the death smell—it went with the job sometimes—but poison gas was another thing entirely. Just as Remo's sense of smell was highly refined, so were his hearing, his vision, his reflexes, and—this was the downside of Sinanju—his susceptibility to irritants that would do no lasting harm to an ordinary person.

"Tell me if it starts getting too bad," Remo said, "and we'll go back. No sense ending up in the hospital if the air isn't breathable yet. According to the TV reports I caught at the airport, the National Guard are still wearing their gas masks."

"The lawyers did not seem affected," Chiun sniffed.

"Lawyers must not breathe the same mixture as you and I."

On either side of the road, stereotypical red barns and tall grain silos marched by. The early-spring breezes toyed with the lush prairie grasses. It seemed all very pastoral to Remo Williams—until he noticed an unusually thick cloud of flies swarming up ahead.

As they passed the cloud, Remo saw directly beneath it stiff hooves pointing up to the sky. He couldn't tell if the hooves belonged to a horse or a cow. Remo was a city boy.

The stench was sour, maggoty. Like rotted meat in old garbage cans. His brow grew worried. If there was any poison gas still in the air, it would be hard to separate from the overripe stink of corruption.

The dead farm animals grew plentiful as they went on.

"I guess this area was downwind of the gas," Remo muttered. "Those poor cows really got it."

"The only good cow is a dead cow," pronounced Chiun, who had no use for beef or dairy products.

"Tell that to the farmers."

Remo noticed a black flag by the road. He assumed it marked a rural mailbox and thought little of it.

But after the third black flag, he started taking notice. They flapped from narrow aluminum poles. The flags were entirely black. There were no mailboxes near any of them. They dotted either side of the road at regularly spaced intervals.

"I don't like the looks of these flags," Remo said. Chiun declined to reply. All through the trek west, he had selectively responded to Remo's comments, evidently reacting only to those he deemed part of the assignment.

The farms flew by. Although the terrain tended toward flatness, the land rolled gently, so it was impossible to see more than a half-mile ahead.

The road must have been a snake track originally, because it whipsawed unexpectedly. Thus Remo wasn't aware of the clot of people clustered at the roadside until he was almost on top of them.

They huddled under a spreading hickory tree, their hair matted, their bodies as ripe, if their body odor was any gauge, as thousand-year-old Chinese eggs.

"Chiun, check this out," Remo said when he saw them.

Grasping the front seat cushions, the Master of Sinanju pulled himself forward to peer past Remo's shoulder. His nails tightened and his tiny mouth dropped open in shock.

"Remo, look at those poor homeless unfortunates," he squeaked. "Reduced to dwelling beneath a mighty tree. Truly, a catastrophe had transpired here."

"I not only see them, I can smell them even through the maggots," Remo said grimly, coasting to a stop.

There seemed to be about a dozen of them, but it was impossible to tell because they blended together into a solid mass of multilegged dust bunnies. One of them pounded away with a hammer. The others held whatever it was they were nailing to the tree.

"Are you people all right?" Remo asked, rolling down the window. He almost gagged. "Can I give you a lift to a shelter?"

"No, we're not all right," the one with the hammer said in a whiny nasal voice. "The frigging pigs threw us out."

"Pigs?" Remo asked, trying to imagine how any

barnyard animals—even if they had survived the gas—could have forced a dozen adults to vacate the town against their will. "Whose pigs?"

"The friggin' Army pigs," the leader snarled. "Who do you think's planting all those useless flags?"

Up close, they looked worse than from a distance. Not only did they resemble ambulatory scarecrows, but their faces were soot black. In fact, their clothes were literally caked with dirt. The man with the hammer turned around. Tangles of hair hung down to his dirty chin, so the front of his head was indistinguishable from the back.

"You're not gas victims?" Remo asked, dumbfounded.

"You hit it right, man. I'm a gas victim. You're a gas victim. We're all going to be gas victims if this friggin' country doesn't wake up to the environmental ecocide going down here! La Plomo is only the beginning. Pretty soon it will be Berkeley, then Cambridge. Then Carmel. Even Martin Sheen won't be able to protect us."

"Remo," Chiun whispered from in back, "drive on. These are not gas victims, but escaped lunatics. I can tolerate having one for a driver, but I will not allow any of these vermin to join me in this vehicle."

"Just a sec," Remo muttered, one hand on the window crank for a quick roll-up. "Did the Army bulldoze you people in a manure pile?" he asked the man with the hammer.

"This isn't manure," the man returned, slapping his khaki jacket. Dust erupted from it in a cloud. The man leaned into the newly formed cloud and snorted it into his lungs greedily. The others joined in, sniffing airborne dirt like dogs.

"Ah," he said. Then he began coughing. "Good

clean dirt!" he hacked. "Mother Nature in her glory! Man, I love it!"

The others began chanting. "Mud is our blood! Our blood is mud!"

From the back seat Chiun's voice came darkly. "I take back what I said, Remo. These *are* gas victims. And it has damaged their brains. Drive on. They are not our concern."

Remo ignored the suggestion. He noticed for the first time that some members of the group wore T-shirts on which a clenched fist was raised in a single-finger salute dimly visible through years of accumulated grime. The shirts were also emblazoned with the words "DIRT FIRST!!"

"You people belong to Dirt First?" Remo asked politely.

"And proud of it, man."

"The same Dirt First!! that spikes trees so that lumberjacks wreck their saws and lose fingers?"

"A finger lasts, what, seventy, eighty years?" the man said, pushing long strands of hair from his face with his grimy thumbs, the better to see. "But a redwood goes on for centuries. Groove on that! Centuries! If that isn't righteous, I don't know what is."

"Believe me," Remo told him, "you don't know wrong from righteous. I notice a hammer in your hand. Don't tell me you're spiking that tree behind you?"

"What's wrong with that?" the stringy-haired man asked belligerently. The others joined in. They sounded like a pack of raucous crows.

"This isn't exactly lumber country," Remo pointed out.

"This oak tree has as much right not to be chopped down as any redwood you could name," he was told. "It's easily a hundred years old, and could live three."

"It's a hickory tree," Remo pointed out. "And what happens if the farmer who owns that tree decides to chop it down?"

"We spray-paint the spike head Day-Glo orange so people know it's spiked."

"That's fine for the next hundred years, but what about after the bark grows over the spike?"

This possibility had apparently never occurred to the members of Dirt First!! They blinked in surprise, causing their eyes to disappear in their blackened faces.

"By that time," the man with the hammer said, "we won't be around to be sued by anybody."

"There's a responsible attitude," Remo said, rolling up his window. He put the car into drive.

"Hey, you reactionary piece of shit!" the Dirt Firster called over. "What about our friggin' ride?"

"Put a tree to good use. Hang yourselves."

Remo put as much distance behind him as fast as the car would take the curves. His last sight of Dirt First!! was in his driver's-side mirror. They were dropping to their hands and knees to suck up his road dust.

"Only in America . . ." Remo muttered.

"Hear, hear," Chiun added, assuming this was a rare acknowledgment of the superiority of Korean culture from his pupil.

"Are we talking again?" Remo asked hopefully.

"No!"

Next they came upon a man urinating into his hand.

He was an Army officer, Remo saw as he slowed the car. He stood at the side of the road behind a long carbon-monoxide-belching line of olive-drab

Army trucks. The trucks blocked the road, forcing Remo to stop.

Remo rolled down the window again and tried not to inhale as he called out to the Army officer.

"Hey, pal, when you're through watering your hand, could you have the trucks pull over so I can get by?"

"You can't get by," said the officer—he was a captain, Remo saw from his collar bars—as he switched hands. He did it without wasting a drop.

"Spoken like a guy with yellow fingers," Remo growled. In a louder voice he called, "I know I can't get by. These trucks are in my way!"

"That's the idea. No civilians allowed. Can't you read the signs?"

"What signs?" Remo asked.

The captain shook a last droplet into his palm and zipped himself up. He rubbed his hands together briskly. He pointed back down the road with a dripping finger.

Remo got out of the car and looked back. He saw no signs. Just one of the black flags lifting and falling in the intermittent breeze.

"All I see is a line of black flags," Remo said.

"Dammit, man. Don't you know an NBC contamination-warning flag when you see it?"

"No, but I know the CBS eye when it's staring me down."

"The black flag," the captain said, "is an NBC contamination warning."

"I heard the media are thick as crows at the attack site, but what good will flags do? They don't frighten that easily."

"NBC," the captain said in a tone of voice usually reserved for potty-training three-year-olds, "stands for Nuclear-Bacteriological-Chemical. Dammit, don't civilians know anything?"

"Just enough not to piss into our hands," Remo said dryly. He noticed the stenciled name on the captain's blouse read: "HOLDEN."

Captain Holden looked down into his hands. He started shaking them dry. Remo took several quick steps backward. "The manual says I gotta do this," Holden muttered. "So what do I do?"

"I'd get a new manual. That one sounds broke."

"Ah, it's all the fault of those Dirt First loonies. They were trudging up the road and I mistook them for walking wounded. When I tried to hose them down, they ran like they never heard of clean."

"New experiences are usually scary," Remo remarked.

"I accidentally sprayed my hands with DS-2," Captain Holden said, jerking his thumb to the stacked cans in the open back of a canvas-covered truck. "The manual says to avoid contamination, you gotta wash your hands quick as you can. When you're in the field without water, the recommendation is to piss on 'em. I know it sounds goofy, but it's the Army way."

"Well," Remo said, gesturing to the tall grasses around them, "you're certainly in the field. One question, though."

"Yeah?"

"If you're carrying poison gas away from the town, why are the trucks pointing toward the town? Or is driving backward as Army as whizzing on your fingers?"

"We're not taking gas from the town. Are you kidding? I wouldn't get near the stuff."

"Then what's in the cans?"

"We're hauling decontaminant solution into the town. Take a look."

The captain went to the open gate of the last truck. As Remo approached, he saw that the stacks of olive-drab canisters were all marked in broken stencil letters: DS-2.

"DS-2?" Remo asked.

"Decontaminant solution two," Holden supplied. "Take a whiff."

The captain unscrewed the khaki cap from one can. A chemical odor roared out, hitting Remo like a freight train. He raced backward to the car before the first cough exploded out of his lungs. He jumped in, saying, "Hang on, Little Father!" Throwing the gears into reverse, he put a good eighth of a mile between him and the corrosive cloud. He screeched to a ragged stop.

"Are you crazy?" Remo shouted through a tiny crack in the window.

The captain replaced the cap and sauntered back, still shaking off his glistening hands.

"Cure's almost as bad as the disease, huh?" he grunted. "Now, if you know what's good for you, you'll skedaddle. We're clearing all civilians out of the decontamination zone."

"Can't. I have business in town," Remo said, sliding a card through the crack. The captain took the card. It read: "REMO BERRY, CRISIS MANAGER, FEDERAL EMERGENCY MANAGEMENT AGENCY."

"FEMA, huh?" Captain Holden said. "Thought you guys weren't due until our job was done." He offered Remo's card back. It was turning yellow around the edges.

"Keep it," Remo said. "Look, I need to get in there."

"Well, I guess we can let FEMA through," Captain Holden said slowly. "But take my advice. Don't stay too long. When we uncork this DS-2, La Plomo ain't gonna be a fit place to breathe."

"Unlike now," Remo said sourly. He closed the window as the captain trudged back to the column of trucks. After a few minutes in which the stink of carbon monoxide from the idling engines insinuated into their car, the trucks started to lurch along, clearing a narrow path.

Carefully Remo slid past them. The captain shot them a hearty wave in passing, sending golden raindrops spattering onto the windshield.

The Master of Sinanju was not silent for long, just as Remo had guessed from his half-baffled, half-horrified expression.

"Remo," Chiun asked in a dim voice as they put the column behind them, "could you explain what that Army man was attempting to accomplish?"

"Gee, Little Father," Remo said airily, "you saw everything that guy said and did. Couldn't you tell?"

4

The town of La Plomo surprised Remo when he laid eyes on it minutes later.

He was expecting desolation or ruin. But the residential section lay pristine and idyllic under the noonday sun, like a brand-new stretch of tract housing awaiting occupation. The maggoty smell was less strong away from the surrounding farmland. The ammonia tang of disinfectants hung low in the air. Although there was a dangerous faint undersmell that might be residual nerve gas, Remo judged the air, if not breathable, nonlethal.

Which was more than the National Guard thought of it, he saw. They stood before a stretch of barbed wire that bisected the road, enveloped in rubberized outer garments, their breath fogging the lenses of their gogglelike gas masks.

Remo pulled off the road and onto a trampled-down cornfield under the shadow of a globular water tower bearing the words "LA PLOMO" in yard-high black letters. On both sides of the road the field was littered with vehicles of all descriptions, from National Guard APC's to mobile TV vans. There was even a limousine with a liveried chauffeur standing by.

Remo turned to the Master of Sinanju, fuming in back.

"Care to chance it?" he asked. "I think it's safe."

"There is no safety in a land where grown men breathe dirt and others urinate into their hands," Chiun intoned. "This is an absurd assignment."

"It can only go uphill from here," Remo said, stepping from the car. The sound of the car door slamming behind him caught the attention of several dozen people doing their best to trample the remaining corn.

Remo was immediately surrounded by a shouting, jostling crowd. Half of them tried to thrust business cards into his hands. The rest shoved microphones into his annoyed face.

"How does it feel to have lost dear loved ones to the horrors of gas warfare?" a man asked.

"Are you going to sue the U.S. government, sir?" inquired a woman.

"If you are, here's my card," a man snapped. "I'm with Dunham and Stiffum, Attorneys at Law."

"Never mind that ambulance chaser," another barked. "Take my card. We're launching a class-action suit."

"Back off," Remo warned, slipping between microphones.

When the crowd only squeezed tighter, Remo began stepping on toes. His right foot snapped out like a jackhammer. Toes crunched and withdrew. Microphones and business cards dropped from fingers. Remo watched as a dozen or so adults suddenly started hopping on one leg, going "ouch, ouch, ouch" in quick, surprised voices. A few fell on their behinds. One man ripped off a shoe and began sucking on a broken toe, cursing and vowing to sue everyone in sight. A dozen business cards settled around him.

"I'm a lawyer myself, idiots," he snarled.

"And I'm with FEMA," Remo said for the benefit of those remaining on their feet.

The microphones snapped back in his face. Instead of business cards, thick folded sheafs of paper were jammed into his hands.

"Here's a subpoena."

"See you in court, murderer."

"You'll rue the day you committed genocide on my client's family."

"Does FEMA have any official reaction to being blamed for this gross miscarriage of trust?"

Remo shredded the subpoenas and shoved the remains into the mouth of the newswoman who had asked the last question.

"Chew on that," he barked.

"Is that a no comment?" she asked, confetti leaking from her too-perfect red lips.

"I don't know, what do you think?" Remo asked acidly.

He stormed off. The crowd parted before him like the Red Sea before Moses. The lawyers especially gave him a wide berth.

Remo looked back to make sure he wasn't being followed and saw the pack regroup and descend upon the Master of Sinanju as he emerged with stately elegance from the car. Remo grinned with expectation.

"Chiun'll send them fleeing for their lives," he chortled.

Instead, the Master of Sinanju tucked his long-nailed fingers into his kimono sleeves like an Oriental wise man and began answering every question put to him.

Remo's face fell. "I don't believe it," he growled. "He's holding a freaking press conference."

Remo decided that was a problem for Smith to

sort out. He started for the barbed-wire perimeter, where a lone National Guardsman held his rifle across his rubberized-fabric chest like a half-melted toy soldier.

"Who's your commander?" Remo asked, flashing a spare FEMA card.

"What say?"

Remo raised his voice. "I said, who's in charge?"

"I can't hear you," the Guardsman said in a muffled voice. "This mask blocks my ears."

"Then take it off!" Remo shouted.

"What?"

Remo reached up and yanked the gas mask off the Guardsman's head. The face beneath turned white. His eyes bugged out.

"My God!" he wailed. "I'm breathing the air!"

"The poison gas is long gone," Remo said impatiently. "Believe me, I know. If it wasn't, I'd be the first to keel over."

But the Guardsman wasn't listening. He made a balloon of his lower face as he desperately tried to recover his mask. Remo dodged his frantic, grasping hands on light feet.

"The air's fine," he repeated.

"It's the smell! I can't stand the smell," the Guardsman gasped. His distended cheeks starting to redden, he shut up.

"Tell me what I want to know and the mask's yours," Remo promised.

"Muff-muggy," the soldier said frantically, pointing to a clot of nearby Guardsmen huddled in conference. They were making wild gestures in a vain effort to communicate with one another.

"The commander's over there?" Remo prompted. "Yes or no?"

"Yes!" the Guardsman gasped. He fell onto the ground, hyperventilating. Remo tossed the mask on his head. Desperately he pulled it over his head and began gulping filtered oxygen.

"What the hell are you going to do if you get into a real combat situation?" Remo asked as the man clambered to his feet.

"Never happen," the Guardsman gasped. "I do this only on weekends. Days, I'm a graphic designer."

Shaking his head, Remo marched over to the group of Guardsmen. To save time, he simply yanked off their masks by way of introduction. Three of them panicked and ran away gagging and clutching their throats. The fourth stood his ground, by which Remo assumed he was in charge. The man's brusque tone confirmed the guess.

"I'm Major Styles," he snapped, "and you'd better have a damned good reason for what you just did."

"Remo Berry, FEMA," Remo said in a bored voice. "I need two questions answered before the Army takes over."

He started. "Army? What Army?"

"The U.S. Army. Who do you think, the Albanian Army?"

"What the hell do they want here?" Major Styles complained. "We secured this pesthole when no one else would touch the job. We were the first authority on station. If you ask me, the Guard was sent in because no one else wanted it. We were practically cannon fodder."

"If you ask me," Remo rejoined, looking at the fleeing Guardsmen, " 'cannon fodder' fits you like a glove."

"I'll have you know that the Guard has a long and honorable history. The Vice-President was a Guardsman."

"I rest my case," Remo said. "Let's stay on the

subject. Anybody suspicious show up after you got here? Maybe someone who wanted to make sure the gas did its job?"

"Everyone suspicious showed up. That's been our biggest headache. Lawyers, newspaper people, TV cameramen, kooks, crackpots—the scum of the earth."

"You're thinking of Dirt First!! maybe."

"I'm specifically thinking of Dirt First!!" the major growled. "We've thrown them out twice. They smell worse than the maggots."

"No argument there. What do you think caused this?"

"Terrorists. It's gotta be terrorists. It smacks of a full-scale military operation. They used Lewisite."

"Lewisite?"

"An old kind of poison gas. Potent stuff. Smells like geraniums. One lungful, and inside of ten minutes, a man would drown in his own blood."

"Any idea how the stuff was introduced?" Remo asked.

"Not a clue. With the right equipment, you can sometimes sniff out hidden ejectors and valves, but the Guard doesn't have any. Maybe the Army will."

"I've got a pretty good nose," Remo remarked dryly. "Mind if I follow it?"

Styles laughed until his mustache bristled. He smoothed it down, saying, "Nobody has that good a nose."

"Humor me. I need to look around the town anyway."

"Come on, then."

Major Styles escorted Remo over the barbed wire and up a pastoral sugar-elm-lined avenue. Remo noticed dead birds lying here and there, partially consumed by flies.

"Smell anything?" Styles asked grimly.

Remo picked up his pace. "Yeah. Geraniums. Over to the left."

They turned left and found themselves in the town square—that was exactly the word for it—where a battered jet fighter sat placidly on a grassy knoll across the street from a strip of boarded-up storefronts.

"Did it crash?" Remo asked.

"No," Major Styles explained. "This here's what passes for a La Plomo monument. They tell me they tried to get a steam engine placed here, but it was no sale. Somebody donated this Sabrejet instead. It dates back to the Korean War. They say the town kids used it for a jungle gym."

"It looks it," Remo said, noticing the dents and initials scratched into the skin. On one wing was etched a heart circling the legend "W.M. Loves D.G. 1991."

When the significance of the graffito sank in, neither man said anything. Then Remo remembered what had drawn him to the aircraft.

Sniffing the air, he followed the infinitely minuscule geranium-like aroma around to the tailpipe. Styles trailed curiously.

"Do me a favor and reach inside," Remo suggested, keeping a respectful distance.

"Why should I?"

"Because you're wearing gasproof gloves, and I'm not."

Shrugging, Major Styles sank to his knees and peered into the tailpipe. His eyes widened comically.

"God damn!" he exclaimed. He reached in and pulled out three fat canisters strapped together by bands of tin flashing.

"Now we know where the gas came from," Remo said flatly.

"They had canisters of the stuff hidden in the tailpipe," Major Styles mumbled in a disbelieving voice. "How about that?"

"Have those tanks shipped to Washington," Remo directed. "And make sure nobody smudges any fingerprints."

"I'll leave it here until someone comes for it. This is outta my league."

"You said it, not me."

They started back for the barbed wire.

"The way I see it," Major Styles was saying, "the Iraqis hid the tanks in the middle of the night and one of their agents just turned the petcocks on the canisters."

"What makes you say Iraqis?" Remo wanted to know.

"Who else would be crazy enough, bloodthirsty enough, and is known to deploy poison gas against innocent noncombatants?"

"The Libyans," Remo said firmly.

"Libyans?" Major Styles snorted. "Hell, what would they be doing in Missouri?" He pronounced it "Missoura," which told Remo he was a native.

"Good point," Remo said with a straight face.

"I tell you none of us are safe in this infernal post-cold-war world. The Russians would never have stooped this low. You should have seen all those glassy-eyed corpses they hauled out of here. Stacked like cordwood, they were. Brrr. Gives me the shivers just thinking about it."

The grumble of motorized trucks broke the stillness.

"That'll be your Army," Styles said edgily. He hesitated, fingering his mustache as if it gave him comfort. "Well, come on. Damn. I've never had any truck with the Army. They're real military."

Remo shot the major a reassuring smile.

"Don't sweat it," he said. "I've met the captain in charge of the detail. Not only do you outrank him, but he's a personable kind of guy."

"Glad you hear it. How do you think I should approach him, protocol-wise?"

"When you shake his hand," Remo advised, "keep your gloves on."

The Army trucks formed a circle in the road just short of the barbed wire. Soldiers jumped out. A squad of them, carrying black flags, deployed in all directions, screwing the flags into every soft-ground surface. When that mission was concluded, the cornfield resembled a golf course in mourning.

Under the direction of Captain Holden, two men lugged various pieces of heavy equipment off the backs of the trucks, among them a pair of gas-powered compressors and another contraption Remo didn't recognize.

When the captain reached over and hit a switch on the latter, Remo concluded it was a portable Klaxon. The deafening short blasts piercing his sensitive eardrums made that a safe deduction. Even the gas-masked Guardsmen were forced to clap their hands over their ears to keep out the strident wailing.

"What the hell are they trying to do, deafen us?" Major Styles barked, hastening forward.

He could have saved himself the exertion, because, unseen by even the soldiers standing around the Klaxon with their hands reaching up protectively into their helmets, the Master of Sinanju floated up to the Klaxon and clapped his hands three times delicately, as if trying to swat a mosquito buzzing the Klaxon horns.

The piercing caterwauling stopped after the last clap.

The soldiers dropped their fingers from their ears and looked to the silent Klaxon. They saw the frail form of the Master of Sinanju leaning thoughtfully over the now-mangled sound horns, which had had the misfortune to be caught between Chiun's hands when he had clapped them.

"What the hell happened?" a soldier demanded.

"I believe this instrument has stopped functioning," Chiun said in a worried tone.

"Must be the battery," Captain Holden said, striding up.

"Yes, it is probably the battery," Chiun said sagely. "It sounds exactly like battery trouble."

"It doesn't sound like anything at all," Holden complained.

"I would not complain about that," Chiun said, floating away. "It is much more pleasing this way."

Remo joined him. "Nice move, Little Father. How'd your little news conference go, by the way?" he asked dryly.

"You may catch the film at eleven," Chiun sniffed.

"And you may catch hell from Smitty," Remo shot back. "You know how he is about us appearing on TV."

"I will not appear on TV in my secret capacity of royal assassin, but as a wronged parent."

"You told them that you were pissed at me?" Remo asked, aghast.

Chiun smiled thinly. "They were most receptive. And sympathetic."

"Did you perchance tell them why you have a bee in your bonnet?" Remo inquired.

Chiun gestured at his bald head. "I am wearing no bonnet."

"Answer the question."

"Yes."

"So will you tell me what's eating at you?"

"You may learn this on the eleven-o'clock news like everyone else," Chiun said haughtily.

Remo's retort was drowned out by a new noise. The discordant clamor of banging metal. Remo looked over to the circle of Army trucks. There, a trio of soldiers was walking around in a circle, helmets tucked under their armpits, banging on them with sticks.

"Oh, what the hell are they doing now?" Remo asked in exasperation.

"It is obvious," Chiun said.

"Not to me," Remo said.

"They are driving the evil spirits away. This is the recommended method."

"This is lunacy," Remo said. "Come on."

The National Guard commander, trailed by a group of his men, had finally mustered up gumption enough to confront the Army captain. He was trying to make himself heard over the noisy racket.

"I'm Major Styles, Captain. May I ask why your men are banging on their helmets?"

"This ought to be good," Remo said to Chiun.

"Because the damn Klaxon's down!" Captain Holden screamed. "The manual specifically says if no warning siren is available, beating on pots or pans or other metal objects is the recommended procedure."

"But the gas is long gone."

"Then why are your men wearing masks?" Captain Holden shot back.

"Can I break in here?" Remo put in. The captain

and the commander looked in his direction. Their eyebrows formed identical regulation arches.

"What is it?" Captain Holden asked sulkily.

"Throw out the manual."

"Is he crazy?" the captain asked the major.

"I hadn't thought so until now, but it's possible. No offense," the major added for Remo's benefit.

"Tell him what the manual says about pissing into your hands," Remo told the captain.

Captain Holden assumed a blank expression. "I haven't the faintest idea what he's talking about, do you?" he undertoned to the major.

"No," Major Styles whispered back. "Is he dangerous?"

Remo threw his hands in the air. "I give up. Listen, you two work out your differences. Just stop that racket until I leave, okay?"

Captain Holden turned to his parading men. "Okay, stop the banging," he ordered. "The civilians should have cleared out by now. The black flags and Klaxons will take care of that."

"What is that man babbling about, Remo?" Chiun asked when Remo returned.

"He thinks the Army manual for gas-warfare emergencies is required reading in every home."

"I have not read it. Have you?"

"Hardly!"

"And neither have they, it seems," Chiun said, pointing to the group of cameramen and reporters clustered around a blue pickup truck.

The sight of the media representatives made Remo realize that they hadn't descended upon the Army, which was strange, he thought.

"Let's check into this, shall we?" he suggested to Chiun.

"Why?"

"The way I figure it," Remo said as they walked

along, "whoever did this is kinda like an arsonist. He's bound to come back, if he hasn't already, to smell the smoke."

"Then you do not think it is terrorists?"

"Do you?"

"No. Terrorists would have announced their barbarism to the world. There have been no announcements."

"Exactly," Remo said, drifting up to the outer edge of the crowd.

It was a big crowd—virtually everyone not in uniform had surrounded the truck. Video cameras pointed up like glass-eyed howitzers. Microphones strained to catch every word spoken by the person standing in the pickup truck's bed.

"Nuclear proliferation is the greatest threat to peace the world has ever seen," the speaker proclaimed in a high, on-the-edge-of-nervous voice.

She was about twenty or twenty-one, wearing faded jeans and a red-and-white-checked workshirt that accentuated her athletic shapeliness. Behind old-fashioned rose-tinted granny glasses, her eyes glowed feverishly. A leather thong circled her forehead, imprisoning her hair, which she wore long and parted precisely down the middle of her scalp. She lifted a clenched fist in righteous anger, causing a silver-and-turquoise Indian necklace to clink on her clavicle.

"You think La Plomo is a fluke?" she shouted. "It's not! La Plomo is just the beginning of a long nightmare in which none of us will be safe. First it was pesticides. Then acid rain. Then poison gas. Next it will be nuclear bombs. Once the pigs let the technology out of the bag, nothing can contain it. I've traveled halfway across the country to give the world my message."

"Can you tell us who you are?" a newswoman asked plaintively.

"No nukes are good nukes," the girl went on, so busy shouting her message she didn't hear the question.

"She sounds like those Dirt First!! dirtbags," Remo muttered.

"They do not think so," Chiun sniffed.

Remo noticed that the contingent from Dirt First!! had returned. They clustered under a decaying apple tree, shouting, "Mud is our blood! Our blood is mud!" in an obvious attempt to get the attention of the media. They were ignored.

"Birds of a feather quarrel together," Remo said.

"At least she does not smell like them," Chiun pointed out.

"Small consolation."

A florid-faced man bumped into Remo. Remo had noticed him as he made the rounds of the crowd. He wore an expensive if flashy suit with a diamond ring on his left little finger. Remo pegged him as a used-car salesman who had come into money.

"Here," he said, flashing Remo a toothy smile. "My card."

Remo ignored the card. "I have all the lawyers I need."

"How about property? I'm in property."

"I just paid off the mortgage," Remo growled, trying to see past the man's meaty expansive features to the girl in the pickup truck.

"It's never too late to trade up," the toothy man pressed.

"I will take one," Chiun said, reaching up. He took the card as the man continued to work the crowd.

Remo's attention returned to the girl on the pickup truck.

"Can you at least give us your name?" a newsman demanded. Remo recognized him as a notorious network anchor famous for changing his sets, clothes, and signoff in an effort to boost his ratings—but never considered learning to polish his frenetic delivery.

"Sky," the girl shouted. "I'm Sky Bluel. From the University of California."

"Did you hear that?" a newswoman next to Remo whispered to another. "She's a UCLA professor."

"That's not what she said," Remo pointed out. "She looks like a student to me."

The newswoman gave Remo a frigid look. "And what station and/or paper are you with?"

Remo, who had never before heard anyone use "and/or" in ordinary conversation, replied, "I'm with the diction police."

"Well, I happen to be with CNN." She turned away as if that was the end of that, thank you very much.

"Remo!" Chiun hissed suddenly, tugging at Remo's sleeve. "Stop that man."

The Master of Sinanju was pointing into the crowd. His face was drawn with concern.

"What man?" Remo asked, one eye on Sky Bluel, who was trying to be heard over the taunts of "Media hog!" coming from the Dirt First!! clique.

"He is an impostor!" Chiun hissed.

"What are you talking about?" Remo said distractedly.

"That man said he was in property," Chiun insisted. "This card proclaims otherwise."

Remo looked down. Chiun held the card up to his nose.

The card read:

"Connors Swindell,
Condominia."

"He's a condom salesman?" Remo said, blinking.

"Exactly. He lied. This is just like your false cards, which lie for you."

"Shhh. Not so loud," Remo hissed, pushing the card away. "Take another look. Condominia must have something to do with condos. He must be a condo salesman."

"If that is true, how do you explain this?"

Chiun turned the card over. Velcroed to the back was a silver-foil packet with the same printing as the card itself.

Remo blinked, Sky Bluel momentarily forgotten. He took the card. The foil pack was, as he had thought, a condom packet. To make sure, he ripped it from the card and opened the packet.

The rolled yellow ring was unmistakably a condom. In fact, Remo's sharp eyes spotted a pinhole defect in the circle of lambskin stretched within the ring.

"So?" he said, shrugging. "He moonlights. Everyone knows condos are as dead as junk bonds." Not wanting to litter, Remo looked around for a proper place to deposit the defective rubber. The CNN newswoman's half-open pocketbook was the most convenient. Unnoticed, he slipped it inside.

Up on the truck bed, Sky Bluel continued to answer questions.

"What is your message, Professor Bluel?"

"I represent a return to the sanity of the sixties,"

Sky Bluel proclaimed. "I speak to the apathetic generation, challenging them to pick up the torch of our sixties mothers and fathers. It's not too late for us to shake up the world. And I speak to the unborn generations who are crying in the darkness, pleading to be born into a world without nuclear weapons."

"What rubbish," Remo snorted.

"What wisdom," Chiun sniffed, brushing a speck of moisture from one eye.

Remo looked down to the Master of Sinanju with an incredulous expression on his high-cheekboned face.

"She speaks eloquently of family values," Chiun explained.

"I speak most of all to the progressive elements of today," Sky Bluel continued, "who can further my cause."

"What cause?" a voice asked politely.

"The unnuking of America!" Sky Bluel cried. "What happened in La Plomo happened because barbarians got hold of the bankrupt and outlawed technology of poison gas. It is too late for the children of La Plomo. But it is not too late for the rest of us."

"Could you explain unnuking?" the notorious anchorman asked.

"I'll do better than that. I'll demonstrate it."

Sky Bluel stepped back to the low, rounded shape behind her. A white tarpaulin smothered it like a huge Gypsy crystal ball under a cloth.

Unhooking the guy wires that kept the tarp from being blown away, she clambered behind the shape, reached down, and like a parlor magician pulling a tablecloth out from under a place setting, whipped the tarp off.

The videocams surged closer. Still photographers

snapped pictures. The lights reflected off a large silver sphere whose stainless-steel surface was a mosaic of circular indentations. It rested on a thick rough-cut wooden board studded with electronic assemblies.

The crowd "oohed" and "aahed" as they recorded the strange object for their news directors.

This went on for two full minutes, until someone thought to ask a question.

"It makes a great visual, Professor Bluel. But exactly what is it?"

"It's a neutron bomb," Sky Bluel said matter-of-factly.

This statement took possibly twenty seconds to sink in. Twenty long seconds while the videocams whirred and the still flashbulbs popped spasmodically.

Remo sensed the prereaction shift in the mood of the crowd before they themselves were aware of it.

"Come on, Little Father," Remo hissed. Getting no answer, he looked to his left. Chiun had already stationed himself well away from the crowd. He regarded Remo with a "What are you waiting for?" twinkle.

Remo stepped out of the way just in time to avoid the stampede.

"Neutron bomb! She's got a live neutron bomb!"

The crowd broke in every direction.

"I do not recall her saying it was live," Chiun remarked to Remo as they watched the crowd scatter.

"She didn't," Remo said.

The Master of Sinanju lifted an inquisitive eyebrow.

"They're reporters," Remo explained.

"Ah," murmured the Master of Sinanju, understanding.

* * *

Up on her pickup flatbed, Sky Bluel stood proudly before her neutron bomb. Her attractive face fell as her audience fled.

"Wait a minute," she complained. "I'm not through rapping yet."

"Oh, yes, you are," a surprise voice in her ear said.

Sky turned. Behind her, somehow, was a tall man in a white T-shirt with dark deepset eyes that made her go blank.

"Wow!" she said. Then, recovering, "Who . . . who are you? I mean, what's your bag, man?"

"I ask the questions. You answer them. Is this thing really live?"

"Sorta."

"Straight answers."

"The shaped charges are real, but there's no isotope in the core. That means it can explode, but it can't achieve critical mass and release hard radiation."

The man in the T-shirt was examining the device critically. "Where the hell did you get it?" he asked.

"I built it."

"You built a neutron bomb?" Remo Williams asked incredulously. "You!"

"That's the whole point," Sky said defensively. "If I can jury-rig one, so can any terrorist."

"We'll argue about it later. How do you disarm this thing?"

"Just pull out the charges by the handles."

Remo looked over the steel ball. Each oversize dimple—it reminded him of a big tennis ball—cupped a handle. Remo counted roughly thirty handles. Each handle bore a simple keyhole.

He looked over to Sky. "Just pull. Is that it?"

"Yeah, like opening drawers." She shook a tiny silver key that hung on a braided chain from her neck. "I didn't bother locking them."

"Sounds too simple."

"That," said Sky Bluel impatiently, "is my point exactly."

Remo called down to Chiun, who had drawn close. He was looking up at them with the cocked head of an inquisitive puppy dog.

"Better get back, Little Father," Remo suggested. "Just in case. I'm dealing with dangerous stuff here."

"I was dealing with dangerous stuff before you were born," the Master of Sinanju snapped. But he retreated to a reasonably safe distance anyway.

"You go with him," Remo snapped to Sky Bluel.

"Don't be ridiculous. I know more about this than you."

Remo took Sky by the wrist, spun her like a square-dance partner doing a do-si-do, and propelled her off the truck with an ungentle shoe in the behind.

Momentum carried Sky Bluel running to Chiun's side.

Remo grabbed the top handle and lifted it straight up. He exposed a long wire-frame cone with a blunt end. A white claylike substance bulged through the wire-frame mesh. The chemical scent of plastique tickled Remo's nostrils. Carefully he set the blunt cone off to one side. The second cone came out more easily. Gaining confidence, Remo went through the rest.

When he was finished, all that was left of the neutron bomb was a skeletal sphere of stainless-steel rings with a grayish metal basketball suspended at its core by struts.

"See? I told you," Sky Bluel called over to him. "Harmless."

But Remo wasn't listening to Sky Bluel. His attention was focused beyond her on the dark figures slinking up to the Army trucks. They had formed a human chain under the noses of the Army—who were preoccupied with firing up a stubborn compressor—passing canisters of decontamination solution two from man to man like a turn-of-the-century fire brigade.

"Damn," Remo growled. "If it isn't one thing, it's another!"

5

Fabrique Foirade grinned as the DS-2 canister was thrust into his broken-nailed hands. He took the sloshing canister and twisted his bony hips. Momentum carried the heavy container to the next and last man in line.

The container left his hands. Chortling, he pivoted back to receive the next one.

Because Fabrique Foirade, treasurer of Dirt First!!, wore his hair over his face like an unkempt Pekingese, his field of vision was not what it should have been. This forced him to work by feel.

So it was by feel that he knew something had broken the chain he had so carefully set up to liberate the dangerous DS-2 solution from the pig ecocide Army. He accepted the next container, and as he horsed it around, it came back at him, almost knocking him off his feet.

"Oof! What's this?" he asked, dumbfounded.

"New game plan," an unfamiliar voice hissed. "We're returning the empty cans so the Army won't know they're gone."

"The pig Army, you mean," Fabrique said reflexively.

"Right, right," the other said vaguely.

Behind his matted curtain of hair, Fabrique Foirade blinked. His eyelashes caught painfully in his hair. He shook the can. It made a heavy sloshing noise.

"This ain't empty," he said.

"I replaced it with pond water. Now, pass it on."

"Hey, who're you, giving me orders? I'm in charge."

"Okay," the other said reasonably. "Let the Army catch us."

"You gotta point there. Okay, keep working."

The cans came back from the truck, and just as quickly, they returned to it. Fabrique, grinning wolfishly and exposing green-stained teeth, chortled with pleasure. He hadn't had this much fun since they burned down the sawmill in Oregon, throwing over two thousand lumberjacks out of work but saving the last habitat of the freckled mudwhacking goldfish, the only pond creature known to masturbate while free-swimming, and therefore of inestimable value to an ecosystem increasingly threatened by undeserving humankind.

"I think this is the last one," whispered the man ahead of him in line after he passed along a can that Fabrique could barely heft because his arms had grown unbelievably tired.

"I think this is the last one," he told the man in charge of replacing the DS-2 with pond water.

"Good," he said. "Give me a second while I dump it out."

"Hey, I just had a thought."

"Treat it kindly, it's in a strange place," the voice offered.

"What's that, man?"

"Here's the can back," the voice said, suddenly chipper.

Groaning, Fabrique Foirade took the can and passed it back.

"Okay, done," he said, panting. "What are you putting the bad stuff in?"

"Back in the truck, where it belongs, of course," the voice said reasonably.

This time the voice struck Fabrique as very strange. For one thing, he hardly coughed at all. No one who belonged to Dirt First!! did not cough. It was impossible. Like being clean.

Fabrique reached up to his curtained-off face and pulled the fall of tangled hair apart. It sounded like cheesecloth ripping. Finally, he uncovered his eyes.

The man standing behind him definitely did not belong to Dirt First!! he saw. For one thing, you could see the natural color of his skin. His face was well-scrubbed. His bare arms were lean, but muscular. His eyes, however, looked weird. Amused, they had a kind of deathly look in them. Like a grinning skull. The guy was sure grinning. He looked like he brushed his teeth at least once a week. Maybe more.

"You, you're the reactionary who—"

The grin squeezed down to a mean, menacing grimace.

"The only reason I don't break every bone in your body," the grinning reactionary warned, "is that to do so I'd have to touch you."

"You afraid of a little honest dirt?" Fabrique sneered.

"No, I'm afraid my hands would stick to your skin forever. It's a terrifying thought."

"Look, man. We're doing the world a favor here."

"You wanna do the world a real favor? Take a bath."

"You don't understand."

"And I don't want to. Pull your troglodytes out of here. How'd you sneak back, anyway?"

"There's more than one road into La Plomo, dude."

"Then you have your choice of exits. Scram."

"You'll be sorry."

"Maybe. But I'll be clean and sorry."

The clean dude stood back, folding his arms. Fabrique Foirade huddled with his followers. After the last of them had received the bad news with a sulky "Bummer!" he led them away from the cluster of Army trucks.

"We should've spiked him, man," a voice complained.

Remo Williams watched them go. He licked his index finger and lifted it into the wind. When the dry side gave him an accurate downwind fix, Remo hurried upwind.

His course took him beyond the Army trucks and into the area where microwave TV vans and press cars were parked haphazardly. Remo stopped, noticed no sign of the media anywhere, and drifted around to the opposite side of the cars.

There the media were hunkered down, trembling and wide-eyed.

"You can come out now," Remo sang.

"What's happening?" someone asked. It was the CNN newswoman. Remo detected a strong smell of urine coming from her general vicinity.

"Nothing," he told her nonchalantly. "The bomb was a dud."

Evidently this possibility had not occurred to any of them, because they took turns saying, "Oh!" in surprised voices.

The press got themselves together. Combs came out. Lipstick and mascara were freshened. The air became sweetly sick with the scent of dozens of brands of ozone-depleting hair sprays. The CNN newswoman disappeared into a microwave van to change underwear.

One network anchor—famous for doing stand-up reports on the war in Afghanistan from the safety of the Pakistani side of the border—was heard to complain that he shouldn't have to spray his own hair.

"How can I be expected to watchdog the environment if I have to fix my hair every five minutes?" he complained bitterly.

The percussive machine-gun sound of the compressors firing up made the air around them shake. The anchor dropped to his stomach, crying, "Incoming!" The others scrambled to follow suit.

"What was that? What was that?" they cried, wild-eyed.

"You're reporters," Remo said, heading back to the Army trucks. "You figure it out."

Under the direction of Captain Holden, the Army was hooking up spray devices to the compressors. Wearing mouth filters, Army privates poured DS-2 into glass-bottle reservoirs. Then, dragging them through an opening they had clipped in the barbed wire over the high-pitched objections of the National Guard commander, they began the decontamination procedure.

With the compressors stuttering like jackhammers, they surrounded the house, a neat white clapboard dwelling with an attached garage.

Captain Holden lifted his hands. "Ready," he shouted.

The spray guns snapped up on six khaki shoulders.

"Aim!"

The spray guns' nozzles dropped into line.

"Fire!"

"Why do they say 'Fire' when they are cleaning that house?" Chiun wanted to know. Remo hadn't heard the Master of Sinanju steal up behind him. Chiun was the only human being on earth stealthy enough to accomplish that feat.

"Search me," Remo muttered. "Where's Moonbeam, the Mad Bomber?"

"I do not understand why you call her that."

"And I don't understand why you think she's so wonderful," Remo snapped back.

"She cares about the children. No doubt she is kind to her parents as well," Chiun added darkly. "Unlike some."

"Are you saying I—"

Their incipient argument was lost in the gush of DS-2 as it hissed and splashed against the side of the house. The solution was dark blue, not much different from liquid household detergent. In fact, after splashing off the house, it left a sudsy residue on the ground.

The house quickly turned light blue. Then dark blue. Then, it seemed to Remo, it began to brown.

"Must be powerful stuff," Remo muttered.

The smell forced them back, so they were never quite sure what happened after that.

Someone yelled, "Fire!" It sounded like Captain Holden's voice. And it was agitated.

"We *are* firing, Captain," a soldier protested.

Remo blinked. The white house—it was now as brown as German chocolate cake—was actually smoldering. It took a second for Remo's eyes to discern that. The hissing foam splashed everywhere, making it hard to see the wisps of smoke. Then he noticed that the once-white paint was bubbling and darkening like burning milk.

The air soon filled with acrid fumes.

"Retreat! Retreat! We used too much!" Captain Holden screamed.

Abandoning their sprayers, the Army unit surged

back from the now-burning house, holding their air filters to their mouths.

"We'd better get back too, Little Father," Remo warned.

The Master of Sinanju faded back from the stinging cloud. A swelling yellowish genie, it billowed madly in all directions.

They passed the press on their way to safety. The press was charging the smoldering ruins, their eyes shiny like drug addicts'.

"A story! This is great! This is wonderful!" they cried.

"This is madness," Chiun said acidly.

"If they want a ringside seat, let them have it," Remo growled. He pointed to the sheltering cornfield, adding, "Let's try there."

They plunged into the spring corn, which was low but thick.

It proved to be a bad idea, because the field was where Dirt First!! had found shelter.

"Not you again!" Remo barked, holding his nose.

"We were here first, man." It was the group's leader, Remo saw with distaste. With his tattered curtain of hair hanging open, he looked like a sheepdog that had survived a head-on collision with a Mack truck.

"You've just been evicted," Remo snapped.

"No fair. Look what they did to that house. You see what we're talking about? The pig ecociders don't know how to coexist with the environment."

Remo looked back at the house. It was now fully engulfed in flames. It seemed to be melting as much as it was burning.

"This DS-2 stuff is so toxic they have to store it in concrete bunkers," the Dirt First!! protester was saying. "Can you dig it, man? The stuff they use to clean nerve gas off their tanks is as hazardous as the gas itself. Un-fucking real."

"I hate to say it," Remo admitted, "but you have a point."

"Right on. I got a membership blank somewheres on me. Interested?"

"You also reek," Remo added. "Now, vamoose."

"Yes," Chiun put in sternly, "do what my son says, malodorous ones. Papoose."

The Dirt Firster put his hands on his hips. "Make me," he said defiantly.

Remo stepped away to give the Master of Sinanju room to work. Chiun regarded the Dirt First!! spokesman with steely eyes. One long-nailed hand drifted up to the man's tangled locks.

Chiun described a short sideways motion, and something plopped to the ground at the Dirt First-er's grimy feet.

He looked down. And saw three years of hirsute growth piled on his dirty boots like a stepped-on tarantula.

"My hair!" he howled in anguish.

"Your life next," Chiun warned.

"I'm gone."

Complaining bitterly, Dirt First made a disor-derly retreat through the spring corn. The corn rows turned black as ruffle-feathered crows in their wake.

"Amazing," Chiun muttered, watching them go. "No matter how much dirt rubs off them, they remain as sooty as chimney sweeps."

"There's nothing amazing about dirt," Remo scoffed, looking around. The media had gotten as close to the conflagration as possible and were film-ing madly. The Army and the National Guard were huddled behind the Army trucks. They were joined by Sky Bluel and a few unidentified people, including, Remo noticed, assorted lawyers and the flashy condo salesman—or whatever he was.

"Did you ever see such a mess, Little Father?" Remo asked.

"No. And why do you not do something about it?"

Remo grunted derisively. "Like what? Step up to the flames and blow them out like Clark Kent?"

"The fire will spread to other houses and soon the entire town will be destroyed," Chiun warned.

"Will anybody care? Let's face it, the townspeople are all dead."

"That man cares," said Chiun, drawing Remo's attention away from the disintegrating house with one long-nailed finger.

It was the supposed condo salesman. He was practically having a fit, and taking out his frustration on Captain Holden.

Remo tuned out the surrounding noise and focused on what the man was shouting.

"That's a ninety-thousand-dollar starter home going up in flames, you moron!" he was screaming. "Why don't you do something before that charming split-level ranch house next to it turns to ash?"

"Sounds like a realtor to me," Remo said.

"He is false, not real," Chiun sniffed.

"Forget it," Captain Holden shot back. "That's a chemical fire. Nothing we can do about it. It's gotta burn itself out."

"Hear that?" Remo told Chiun. "Nothing can be done."

"There is always something," Chiun said, hiking his kimono skirts up. "And we will discover it together. Come."

Reluctantly Remo followed the Master of Sinanju. He stalked close to the fire, skirting the media, which were slowly being pushed back by the heat and dense acrid smoke. Remo wondered what they were going to do with all that footage. They already had enough for a four-hour documentary, and most news reports lasted less than ninety seconds, at least half of which was close-ups of the reporters.

"We can't put that out," Remo said.

"There is always a way." Chiun's voice was firm.

"We'd need Red Adair for this one," Remo said flatly, "and I don't have his number."

Chiun turned. "I am unfamiliar with this Adair the Red."

"He's the guy who snuffs out those big oil-well fires with high explosives," Remo explained. He instantly regretted his words.

"Then we will use explosives," Chiun announced triumphantly.

"Now, where are we gonna get . . . ?" Remo's voice trailed off. "You're not thinking what I *think* you're thinking."

"I do not know what you think I am thinking, Remo, but I am looking in the same direction as you are."

His eyes on the dismantled neutron bomb and its extracted plastique charges, Remo sighed in helpless resignation. "Okay, might as well give it a shot."

They retreated to the pickup truck, picked up two plastique cones by the handles, and started back for the burning house.

Sky Bluel caught sight of this and came running after them, shouting, "What are you doing? Where are you going with my neutron bomb?"

At the sound of the words "neutron bomb," media heads turned as if all on a single pivot. Their eyes grew wide in their smoke-stained faces.

"I'm going to put it to good use," Remo growled. "Now, get back."

"Do you know how powerful those are?" Sky screeched.

"Are they powerful enough to blow that house apart?" Remo asked coolly.

"Definitely," Sky told him.

"Then that's what we're going to do. Now, get back."

Sky, her voice beseeching, turned to the media. "Help me, all of you! They're going to nuke that house!"

That was enough for the media, who had been so petrified by Sky's last statement that they forgot to turn their cameras in the same direction as their frightened eyes.

They broke for the shelter of the Army trucks. Sky, caught between her indignation and her fear of what the plastique charges could do, followed.

"You'll be sorry!" she called.

"We're already sorry," Remo informed her.

Remo and Chiun came to within fifty yards of the burning house. The wind had fortunately changed direction by this time. The worst of the chemical-laden smoke was going west, away from them.

"Okay," Remo said, "I'll throw the first charge. And if we need more bang, you go next."

Chiun frowned. "No. I must have the honor of throwing the first boom. I will not be cheated of this."

"Look, it's probably going to need two hits anyway. How about I go first, we'll see what it does, and you can have the honor of throwing the one that actually suppresses the last of the fire? Sound fair?"

Chiun's hazel eyes squeezed into sly slits.

"That is satisfactory," he said solemnly. "Proceed."

Holding the plastique cone by its convenient handle, Remo hauled back and let fly. He seemed to exert no more force than a man throwing a horseshoe, but the heavy charge lifted, arced, and dropped straight down on the house. It punched a neat hole in the shingled roof.

Nothing happened for a moment.

"Maybe we will need your charge after all," Remo started to say. He looked to Chiun's hands. They were empty. And the Master of Sinanju wore a Cheshire grin that was not mirrored in his pupil's openmouthed face.

"You didn't . . ." Remo started to say.

Then the entire sky turned blinding white, and the world around them shook apart.

6

The house simply ceased to exist.

One moment it was generating more smoke than a coal-burning factory; the next, the sky was raining chimney bricks and flaming shards and the air was full of concussive force.

Remo was blown backward in spite of himself.

The shock wave simply picked him off his feet and bore him back like a giant hand. There was nothing Remo could do, so he surrendered to the force of the compressed moving air.

One heel scraped ground. His shoe came off and skipped away.

Using the other foot because he didn't want to shear the meat loose from the sole of his unshod foot—that was how fast he was flying—Remo tried to brake his headlong flight. He lost that shoe too. And kept going.

Craning his head, he called Chiun's name. There was no answer and no sign of Chiun. His heart dropped into his stomach.

Oh, God, he thought, I've lost Chiun!

His survival instincts took over then.

Remo twisted his body in mid-flight until he could see behind him. The good news was that his trajectory was not threatening to slam him into any of the scattered vehicles, as he had feared.

The bad news was that he was heading straight for a paralyzed cluster of Dirt First!! protesters.

"Might as well go with the flow," he said.

Grabbing at a passing black NBC flag, Remo used it to deflect his flight slightly to the left.

Remo zeroed in on a particularly large and soft woman, who looked like an upright sofa stuffed into an Indian dress. Using his straightened legs like a giant rudder, he arrowed for her.

The woman cushioned the blow surprisingly little. The Dirt Firsters flew apart like stricken tenpins. But Remo kept going.

Frantically he grabbed at passing cornstalks in an effort to slow himself down.

He hit the ground doing over sixty.

Remo rolled and rolled and rolled. And somewhere in the rolling, his head bounced off a half-buried stone and he lost consciousness.

The next thing he knew, Remo was looking up at blue sky. He let his eyes focus on a single solitary cloud that reminded him of Chiun's kind face. It even had a wispy tail of a beard. The Chiun cloud refused to come into focus. Remo concentrated. Then it crystallized into perfect clarity.

In focus, the cloud looked like a hollow-eyed skull.

Remo sat up slowly. Nothing locked or splintered, so he knew that he was okay from the waist up. He felt his legs. No bones broken there. His bare toes stuck up. He wiggled them. All ten wiggled nicely. He was intact. Nothing was broken anywhere.

Only then did Remo jump to his feet.

"Chiun!" he called.

There was no answer.

"Chiun! Where are you?" he cried. Anxiety seized his vitals like cold iron talons.

Remo looked around frantically. Where the white clapboard house had stood was now a vast crater. The house next to it was gone. So were all the others for about eight blocks around. Beyond the zone of destruction, other nearby houses showed damage—broken windows, scars, and like destruction—but they still stood.

It looked to Remo as if a cyclone had picked up the north end of La Plomo and carried it away.

The Army trucks were still in a circle, Remo also saw. But they lay on their sides. The ground around them was littered with the clear grit of their missing windshields. Walking dazedly amid the ruins were Army and National Guard soldiers, poking the blackened rubble with sticks.

Suddenly afraid, Remo raced toward them.

He grabbed one at random. "Chiun—have you seen Chiun?" he asked anxiously.

"What's he look like?" the soldier asked flatly.

"He's the old Oriental. In the gray kimono. He came with me."

The soldier nodded. "Yeah. He's one of the ones we're still searching for."

"Damn! Who else is missing?"

"That kooky psychedelic gal."

Remo looked around. Sky Bluel's pickup was gone. He pointed this out to the soldier. "Looks like she drove off," he said.

"Hey, don't ask me. I still haven't figured out what the hell happened here. One moment we were huddled behind the trucks. The next, there was a flash, and blooey! Everything went."

"Keep looking," Remo said harshly. "People don't just disappear without a trace."

"Why not?" the soldier said reasonably. "All those houses yonder did."

"Just keep looking." And because he was fearful for his Master's fate, he added, "Please."

Remo rushed around the blast area aimlessly, frantic, searching. He found nothing.

Captain Holden accosted him.

"Well, you survived at least," he said grimly.

Remo grabbed him. "Where's Chiun? He's the old Korean. Have you seen him?"

"No, we're still searching for bodies."

"How many so far?" Remo asked in horror.

"None."

Remo's sigh of relief lifted Holden's hair off his forehead. "Then there's a chance. Look, we gotta find Chiun."

"You should sit down and get your wits about you first," Holden said. "You look a mess. The flies won't return for a spell yet. The concussion spooked them good. Any bodies out there can wait."

Eyes narrowing to opaline gems of fury, Remo grabbed Captain Holden by the throat with both fists. He lifted the captain off his feet for emphasis.

"Get your men together," Remo said in a low but violent voice. "You find my friend. Or they'll be looking for your pieces next."

"See here, FEMA can't lord it over a U.S. Army captain."

"Your idiots started that fire," Remo shot back. "You're responsible for what happened." He squeezed hard.

"Anything you say," Holden gasped.

Remo dropped him so fast he loosened the captain's back molars.

Straightening his uniform hurriedly, Captain Holden mustered his men. Under Remo's lashing words, they widened the search area to include the cornfield. Someone wondered aloud what a civilian was doing giving the Army orders. Captain Holden grabbed the man and put his hand over the soldier's mouth and hissed urgent words into his ear until the soldier started nodding his head in furious agreement.

The soldier rejoined the search in a subdued mood. The National Guard pitched in. They ranged far and wide.

The search was filmed extensively by legions of camcorders. Reporters hindered the effort with a steady barrage of questions.

When Major Styles suggested they drop their equipment and join in the search, he was told, "We cover the news, not make it."

When one had the temerity to approach Remo with a "How is the search progressing?", Remo showed him a new way to carry his microphone.

The reporter retreated to his convertible and burned rubber on his way to the nearest proctologist. He drove standing up.

After that, the media kept a respectful distance.

"You have a way with the media," Styles remarked to Remo.

"You just have to find their hot buttons," Remo snapped.

They found the Master of Sinanju among the corn. A delighted Guardsman made the discovery.

"I found him, sir," he shouted, waving wildly.

The search party converged on the spot. Compared to Remo, they were moving in slow motion. Remo flashed through the corn so fast he shucked leaves off the stalks.

"Where is he?" Remo asked as he came up on the Guardsman.

The man pointed to his feet.

Remo stopped dead in his tracks, his gorge rising. The Master of Sinanju lay there on his stomach, bare legs apart under the hiked-up kimono skirt. Chiun's head was turned so one cheek rested in the dirt to show his face in profile.

Shocked by the bloodlessness of his mentor's parchment skin, Remo sank to one knee. A solitary fly crawled out from behind Chiun's shell of an ear. Angrily Remo killed it with a violent snap of his fingers.

Slowly, one outstretched hand trembling, he reached down to touch his Master's throat. He hesitated. The others drifted up, making the cornstalks complain under their feet.

A camcorder approached like an intrusive eye.

"Get back!" Remo snarled, shattering the lens with a swift knuckle blow.

The crowd retreated to a safe distance.

Remo laid a finger against the Master of Sinanju's carotid artery. He felt nothing. His stomach sank. He stifled a sob.

Then the artery pulsed. And pulsed again.

Remo breathed then.

"Thank God," he said chokingly. "You're alive, Little Father. Thank God."

Remo got to work. First he arranged Chiun's skirts so his legs were covered. Chiun had always been modest about his legs showing. Carefully he felt Chiun's arms and legs, testing the birdlike bones for breaks. Finding none, Remo placed his hands on the pale yellow skull, massaging the bone plates to detect cracks or the telltale gravelly texture of crushed bone. He could feel the throbbing of the brain beneath the paper-thin bone.

The skull was fine.

Only then did Remo gently turn Chiun over onto his back.

A hand placed over the delicate mouth picked up regular but soft exhalations. Breathing was normal.

Knowing that there was no major damage, Remo settled down to await the Master of Sinanju's imminent return to consciousness.

"Shouldn't we call an ambulance?" Captain Holden suggested from a discreet distance.

"No!" Remo snapped. And that was the end of that discussion.

A sharper rising of Chiun's small chest gave Remo the first indication that Chiun was coming around. The eyelids began to flutter.

Then, dramatically, Chiun's eyes flew open.

"Remo," he squeaked. "What has happened?"

"Little Father," Remo said solemnly, "I don't know how to break this to you."

Chiun's sweet wrinkles convulsed with surprise. "What is it, Remo?"

"We used too much explosive." And he smiled.

Remo stood up and offered his hand to Chiun. Strangely, the Master of Sinanju rejected it.

"I am not an invalid," he said peevishly. "I can regain my own feet."

"Hey, no offense intended," Remo said, stepping back. "It's just that we both took a pretty heavy hit. I was out too."

"And just because you regained your white senses first, you think you are stronger than I, who taught you everything you know?" Chiun intoned as he came to his feet like an unfolding paper kite. Angrily he brushed off his dusty kimono.

"It's not like that at all," Remo objected. "It's just I—"

"Hey, we found another one!"

A National Guardsman trudged up, leading a

dazed Sky Bluel by the hand. Her rose-tinted glasses hung askew off the bridge of her uptilted nose.

"I thought she left," Remo said, his argument with Chiun momentarily forgotten.

"What made you think that?" Captain Holden asked.

"Because her pickup is gone." Remo pointed to the gnarled apple tree where it had been parked. "Look."

Sky Bluel shook off her dazed look when Remo's words sank in.

"My pickup!" she cried. "My neutron bomb! My science project! They're all gone!"

"What neutron bomb?" Captain Holden asked blankly.

"My neutron bomb, you ninny! Didn't you catch my press conference? I brought it in my pickup. Actually, it's my dad's pickup. And he's going to kill me for losing it."

"Well, it didn't drive off by itself," Remo pointed out. "Anybody see where it went to?"

No one had. They conducted a general search. The truck had not been blown into a ditch, or anything of the sort.

"Maybe it blew up with the rest of the plastique," Remo suggested after they had regrouped in defeat. "There was an awful lot of it in back."

"Don't be a moron," Sky snapped. "I parked it near that apple tree. The tree is still there. If that plastique had gone up, there'd be a crater, not an apple tree." She shook an angry finger in Remo's face. "And none of this would have happened if you hadn't tried to play macho superhero."

"Sue me," Remo said.

Two lawyers trotted up in response, offering their

cards. Remo sent them away, joined at the bridgework.

An hour later, the entire area had been gone over. They found no bodies. No sign of the missing pickup. Only Remo's shoes. Much of the media had left to file stories. The remainder were cowering behind convenient solid objects, fearful of Remo's wrath, writing what they half-hoped, half-feared, would be their final glorious stories, while awaiting the next catastrophic event.

Shod once more, Remo accosted Sky Bluel.

"Let's face it," he said flatly. "Someone stole the truck."

"I know that!" Sky snorted. "I knew it an hour ago. But no one would listen to me!"

"Now we all know it too. So who did it?"

"Search me."

"Anyone you talk to show special interest in the bomb?"

"Nobody seemed indifferent," Sky said bitterly. "I came here to deliver a message to the world, and I caught people's attention, didn't I?"

"Screw your dippy message," Remo said harshly. "Answer my question."

"The media were fascinated, okay? So were the Dirt First people."

"You talked to them?"

"A little," Sky admitted adjusting her granny glasses. They were too big for her narrow face. "They were kinda righteous."

"Not to mention ripe. Anyone else?"

"Let's see, a few outta sight soldiers."

Remo called over to Captain Holden.

"Any of your men missing?"

"No, sir." The "sir" was very respectful.

"What about the Guard?"

"No Guardsmen missing," Major Styles offered.

Remo turned to Sky again. "Okay, who else?"

"Some other people."

"Like who?"

"You know—just people. One guy asked a lot of good, insightful, and even progressive questions, considering he looked awfully square."

"What kind of questions?"

"Oh, stuff about what the bomb affects and what it doesn't. Neutron bombs don't damage cities. They're strictly people-killers, you know."

"Unlike the hydrogen bomb," Remo said dryly. "Was he a reporter?"

"He didn't say. But he did give me his card."

"Let's see it."

Sky searched her jeans pockets. Finding nothing, she showed empty hands and an unhappy face. "I must have lost it in the corn."

"Think. Did he have any distinguishing features?" Remo asked, glancing at the two lawyers who were trying to untangle their bridgework while simultaneously drooling on their ties.

"Come to think of it, he did have this really, really insincere smile."

"Thanks," Remo grumbled. "That really narrows it down."

It took thirty more minutes, but Remo and the others collected every card they could find. They found plenty. Most of them were law-firm business cards. A few belonged to TV people. There were dozens of the condoms mounted on cards, too.

"Was it any of these?" Remo asked Sky.

Fingering the key around her neck, Sky Bluel looked at the mountain of cards the soldiers had piled at her feet.

"Are you kidding me?" Sky asked excitedly.

"At least try," Remo insisted.

"Why should I? Who the hell are you, anyway?"

Remo dug out his wallet and presented her with his FEMA ID card.

Sky looked at it. A distasteful expression crossed her face.

"You're a suit," she said unhappily.

"A what?"

"A U.S. Grade A porker." Sky Bluel threw Remo's card into the pile with contempt and stalked off.

Remo let her go. He looked around him. He saw an idyllic Missouri farm town with a gaping black crater at one end. Tipped-over Army trucks stood around, looking about as useful as the foil-packed condoms decorating the pile of business cards.

And standing a little away from the center of activity, the Master of Sinanju had found a TV newsman who had not yet interviewed him. He was speaking into the microphone with stiff-necked intensity.

"I give up," Remo groaned. "This is too much for me." He went in search of a telephone.

It turned out that electricity and phone service into La Plomo, Missouri, had long ago been cut off. Remo figured this out when the third house he broke into harbored a dead phone.

He went to Captain Holden.

"I need to report in to my boss," Remo said unhappily.

"Good luck. When FEMA finds out you practically blew the north end of the town to pieces, you'll probably need a new line of work."

"Thanks for reminding me," Remo said sourly. "Now, how about that phone?"

"I don't have one."

"Then how do you report in?"

"By field radio."

"Who does that connect to?" Remo asked patiently.

"Fort Wood, down in the Ozarks."

"Can they get a line to Washington?"

Holden squinted one eye. "Theoretically."

"What do you mean—theoretically?"

"One: this is the all-volunteer Army," Captain Holden explained. "Where the impossible is routine, but the ordinary is usually impossible. We can fight wars, ford rivers, and secure positions, but placing a simple phone call can get messy."

"What's two?"

"Two," Captain Holden said, "is even if command can place your call, they won't."

"Why the hell not?"

"Because you're a damn civilian. No offense."

"You'd be amazed what a well-motivated civilian can do at a time like this," Remo said tightly. "Lead me to that radio."

Because he had nothing to lose and was still a little bit afraid of Remo, Captain Holden escorted Remo into the back of one of the few field trucks still upright. A radio set sat on a shelf in back. Holden personally fired the set up and initiated the call to Fort Wood.

A tinny voice crackled out of the microphone presently.

"Fort Wood, go ahead, Echo Leader."

"That's me," Holden said proudly. He cleared his throat. "I got a FEMA guy who wants a patch-through to Washington."

"Tell him to stuff it."

"You tell him," Holden said, passing the microphone to Remo. "I like my bones knit just the way they are."

Remo accepted the microphone. "The number is area code 111-111-1111," he said. "Dial it."

"No can do," the radioman said laconically.

"You got a pair of earphones on?" Remo asked.

"Affirmative."

"Got an extra set for when those break?"

"That's another affirmative."

"Okay, I want you to call me back in five minutes."

"Why?"

"Because that's when your eardrums will be working," Remo Williams said, slipping two fingers into his mouth and emitting a piercingly sharp whistle at the mike.

Captain Holden clapped his hands over his own ears. So he didn't hear the eruption of profanity that emerged from the hissing speaker.

Remo lowered the volume and started counting the seconds. When he got to three hundred, exactly five minutes later, he raised the volume again.

"You back?" he asked politely.

"What was that number, sir?"

Remo grinned. "Dial 111-111-1111 and patch me through. And whatever you do, don't listen in. The other end will be able to tell and he'll inform me and I'm liable to treat you to a really rousing chorus of 'Whistle While You Work.' "

"That's a double-triple affirmative, sir," the radioman shot back. The sound of plugs slipping into jacks came over the mike.

"I never heard of a double-triple affirmative," Captain Holden said wonderingly. "Is that in the manual?"

"Why don't you check?" Remo said over the sound of a phone ringing through the speaker.

Taking the hint, Captain Holden left the truck in a hurry.

The lemony voice of Dr. Harold W. Smith came

over the speaker, sounding like a bad wire recording from circa 1943.

"Yes?"

"This is Remo."

"Let me have your report," Smith said crisply.

"I'm not sure where to begin," Remo offered.

"Have you any suspects or leads?"

"Too many. Got a pencil?"

"Of course."

"Write this down. Dirt First!! That's with two exclamation points."

"The ecoterrorist group?" Smith asked, startled. "They are there?"

"In strength—and I don't mean numbers," Remo added. "Actually, they left after the explosion."

"What explosion?"

"I'm getting to that. Then we have Sky Bluel of the University of California."

"Is that a person or a student organization?"

"More like a throwback to the sixties. But she's female."

"Why is she important?"

"She brought a neutron bomb to the party." Remo's voice was a study in casualness. He was rewarded by a two-octave jump in Smith's tone.

"My God, did it go off?"

"Yes and no."

"Remo, there is no yes-and-no about a neutron bomb. When they go critical, they emit high-speed neutrons in lethal concentrations. Depending on the isotope involved and the size of the device, casualties could be enormous."

"La Plomo is a ghost town, remember? The bomb wasn't primed to send out radiation. Only the plastique charges went up."

"What madman would do that?"

"Actually, I did," Remo said, sudden sheepishness creeping into his tone.

"You, Remo? Why?"

"I was trying to put out a burning building. The Army set it on fire."

"Why would the Army do that? Their job is to decontaminate La Plomo, not burn it to the ground."

"That's exactly how the fire began."

"Remo," Smith said wearily, "this sounds very involved."

"And I haven't gotten to the condom salesman who talked like a realty broker."

"What?"

"Not to mention the media," Remo added. "A representative of which, by the way, is right now doing an interview with Chiun."

"Chiun? He cannot appear on TV. Security could be compromised."

"I don't think he's talking about the organization," Remo said distantly as he cut a slit in the canvas side of the truck with a finger. "The subject for today is his ungrateful pupil."

Smith sighed like a leaky bellows. "He is still angry with you?"

"On and off," Remo admitted, peering through the ragged slot. No one was eavesdropping, he saw. "Right now, it's on."

"Why?"

"Haven't a clue."

"Remo, I am having trouble making sense of your report."

"It's not over yet," Remo said quickly. "I don't know who gassed La Plomo—what's that mean, by the way? The Plow?"

"No, it's Spanish for 'the lead.' The original settlers mistakenly believed it was French for 'the feather.' They thought the surrounding virgin prairie had a feathery look. They discovered their mistake after the town began appearing on area maps. The name was never changed."

"So much for the Show Me state," Remo said dryly. "As I was saying, I don't know who gassed the town, but I think they're still hanging around, because someone made off with that neutron bomb."

"I thought you said it detonated."

"You weren't listening. Only a couple of the plastique charges went up. The bomb casing and the rest of the device are intact—at least the last I saw it, they were."

"Describe this device, Remo," Smith asked urgently.

Remo launched into a complete description of Sky Bluel's device, finishing with, "It looked like a parlor magician's steel hoops—you know, the interlocking rings trick—welded into a ball. After the charges were taken out, that is."

"And you say a USC professor constructed it?"

"A popular misconception. Actually, she's a student. Must be this semester's science project."

Smith was silent for a moment. The speaker hissed and crackled annoyingly. When Smith came back on, he said, "It could work. This woman claimed there was no core?"

"Yep. Made me wonder what the grayish ball in the middle was."

"Hmmm. Probably the beryllium-oxide shielding," Smith mused. "Still, the person who stole it might not have realized that was what it was. This is very suggestive, Remo."

"Not to me. I don't get off on neutron bombs."

"It is suggestive in this way. The neutron bomb is in many ways the nuclear equivalent to poison gas. It is a tactical battlefield weapon, designed to annihilate enemy forces in a target area, without damaging property. A relatively compact blast crater is generated, but nothing on the order of a full-scale nuclear missile."

"So?"

"All along, Remo, our theory has been that whoever deployed that gas did so because it was the cheapest agent of terror available to him or them. But the theft of a neutron bomb—even the presence of one in the death zone—makes me wonder."

"Wonder what?"

"Who would be interested in a destructive device that kills people but does not harm the surrounding area."

"Dirt First!" Remo said, snapping his fingers.

"Exactly, Remo. You and Chiun had best pursue that angle."

"Any suggestions how? They were the only ones who didn't leave business cards."

"Yes. They're based in San Francisco. They're in the book. Go there. Infiltrate the organization, and if you learn Dirt First is responsible for any of this, dismember it from within. After you recover the device, of course."

"Uh, Smitty. I don't think you quite grasp what you're asking me to do."

"I am asking you to do a very simple task—one you've undertaken many, many times," Smith said testily. "Get inside, learn what you can, and do what you can. What is the problem?"

"These people smell."

"That is hardly a hardship," Smith said snappishly.

"They roll in the dirt. They breathe dirt. They exhale dirt. For all I know, they eat the stuff. They're like that *Peanuts* character, Pigpen."

"You will do what you have to, Remo," Smith said sternly. "La Plomo may be only the beginning."

"If you think Chiun is going to take a mud bath for this mission, you are sadly mistaken."

"You will find a way," Smith said. "You always do."

"What about Sky Bluel?" Remo asked.

"I am punching her up on my computer now." Pause. "Yes, she's a student at USC-Berkeley. Resides off-campus. Her parents live in Stockton. Politically active on her campus, but no known affiliations with subversive groups. Take charge of her until we sort this out."

"I'm not a baby-sitter," Remo said tightly.

"And we are no closer to solving this mystery than before you arrived. If what this girl says about her neutron bomb is true, that it is unarmed, then it stands to reason that whoever possesses it may realize that without Sky Bluel, they have stolen a useless shell. They may take steps to rectify this."

"If you say so," Remo said reluctantly. "You know, if all those people hadn't died before we got on the scene, I'd call this the stupidest assignment you ever handed us, Smitty."

"Do not make the fatal mistake of underestimating this one, Remo," Smith said soberly. "Sometimes the ones we do not take seriously are the ones that end up costing us."

"Not this time," Remo said, breaking contact.

Before he could reach for the cutoff switch, the radio operator came on.

"I didn't hear a word, sir. You have my word on that." The voice was so sincere that Remo saved his pungent retort and said only, "Signing off."

He stepped out into the light. He looked around. Captain Holden was standing well away from the truck, leafing through an olive-drab book of some sort. Remo wiggled a finger in his direction.

Holden trotted up. "There's no double-triple affirmative in the manual," he said mournfully.

"Now you know," Remo told him. "Seen Chiun?"

"He's waiting in your car," Holden told him.

"What about Sky?"

"She thumbed a ride a few minutes ago."

"What idiot gave her a lift?"

"I'm not sure. I think he was a TV reporter."

"Think?"

"He looked kinda familiar, but we don't watch much TV in the Army."

"Thanks a whole bunch," Remo growled. He hurried to the car, which, other than a fender scratch from some airborne piece of debris, was intact.

Chiun sat in back, looking severe.

Remo got behind the wheel. He started the engine.

"Tired?" Remo asked solicitously.

"No!" Chiun said vehemently.

"Hey, I was just asking. Settle down. Listen, I just spoke with Smitty."

"I know. Why do you think I so patiently wait here?"

"You were listening in?"

"My hearing is keener than a wolf's. I do not have to eavesdrop. The very wind carries your braying to my perfect ears. I am ready to do as Emperor Smith bids."

"Fine," Remo said, sending the car around in a circle, "because you've got the baby-sitting end of this gig. If we ever find Sky Bluel."

"And you may roll in the mud and eat dirt, which is exactly what I would expect you to prefer."

Remo glowered as he stepped on the gas. He wasn't looking forward to that end of the assignment.

7

Don Cooder was not afraid to go where other anchors feared to tread. Vietnam. Attica. Afghanistan. Baghdad. Anywhere as long as it provided a violent backdrop for a stand-up report and a host of anti-U.S. troops to protect his back.

Cooder, whose rough-hewn outdoorsy looks and forced Texas drawl had made his a household face, took the difficult assignments not because he was the highest-paid anchor in history. The answer was much simpler. He came in a consistent dead last in the ratings.

That being dead last meant that *The Evening News with Don Cooder* was still seen by an estimated ninety million Americans each night mattered little. It wasn't enough. He had to be first. And he would be first, Cooder vowed silently.

Especially after he got an exclusive interview with the brave girl who had built a working neutron bomb to show the unthinking world that anybody, but anybody, could build one in their backyard.

"Incredible," Cooder said as he piloted his Lincoln along the scenic back roads of Missouri. "To think that a mere high-school girl, working with common everyday household articles, could devise a working neutronic bomb."

"Neutron bomb," corrected Sky Bluel, fidgeting beside him. "And I'm a grad student at USC-Berkeley. Not some high-school senior."

"Are you sure?" Cooder asked, touching the distinguished gray at his temples. It took him twenty minutes each night to keep that gray there. It came out of a bottle.

"Of course I'm sure. I know what school I go to!"

Cooder frowned. "You'll have to learn to relax when we go on camera," he cautioned. "You're too hot. Television is a cool medium."

"Hot? I'm furious! Someone stole my bomb. How am I going to make my point without proof? And for the last time, it's not a working bomb. How many times do I have to repeat myself?"

"Not working, huh?" Cooder mused, sensing his rating share dropping like the temperature in September. "But you can build another, am I right? One that works?"

"Sure," Sky admitted. "With the right materials and enough time."

"I can get you the materials. Can you have it by Thursday?"

Sky's perfect hairline jumped up. "Thursday?"

"That's when my news show, *Twenty-four Hours*, airs. What do you think of 'Twenty-four Hours on Neutron Street' for a segment title?"

"We're getting off the wavelength," Sky complained. "You can't build one of these things out of stuff you can get at any hardware store. I'm a physics major. I do my grad work at USC's Lawrence Livermore National Laboratory, you know?"

"Isn't that the place where all those nuclear materials turned up missing last year?" Cooder asked suddenly.

"Right on! Now you're in the groove."

Don Cooder braked the car, his eyes flying wide. Suddenly he saw sitting beside him, not an interview subject that would expose America's run-amok nuclear incompetence, but a cunning thief whom he could accuse on nationwide TV of pillaging important nuclear materials.

"Why are you looking at me like that?" Sky Bluel asked in an uneasy voice.

"Like what?" Cooder said, covering.

"Like you got stars in your eyes all of a sudden."

"Not stars, points."

"Excuse me?"

"Rating points," Cooder explained, the glaze going out of his eyes. "Why don't you tell me your story again?"

"I already have. Weren't you listening?"

"I'll listen harder this time," promised Don Cooder, reaching into his silk suit for a tiny bottle of hair spray. He ran a jet of it around his crowning glory of wavy black hair.

"That stuff burns holes in the ozone, you know," Sky said disapprovingly.

"My five-part story on the rape of the Amazon rain forest saved an estimated ten thousand trees," Cooder shot back in his best indigant on-air tone. "I did one of the first network features on saving the hunched back whales. It raised America's consciousness by an estimated three share."

"Oh yeah? For your information, it's humpback whale, and what's that got to do with hair spray?"

"Anchors make news. Hair makes anchors. And hair spray makes anchors' hair. I think a little depleted ozone is worth all the beneficial consciousness-raising that I do, don't you?"

Sky blinked behind her granny glasses. "Put that way, yeah," she said vaguely. "It does sorta make sense. Vaguely."

"It's a sensible world," Cooder said. "Now, from the top."

"I was working with fissionable materials at Lawrence Livermore," Sky began, "doing—"

"They let a girl do that?" Cooder exploded.

"I happen to be brilliant. I was born in the Age of Aquarius. Anyway, what I found appalled me. Security is unbelievably sloppy. It was easy to filch stuff. People were doing it all the time."

"But you didn't filch any nuclear material?"

"Nah, I just took enough stuff to make the bomb casing."

"Could you?"

"Sure. Anytime. But why would I want to?"

"To show the world!" Don Cooder trumpeted. "You show them that if you can do it, anyone can."

"But that is what I'm doing," Sky protested. "I built a working birdcage—that's techtalk for the bomb casing. Plastique charges, beryllium-oxide tamper—the works! I don't technically think I need to have any fission-material stuff in the bomb to make my case to the Izod generation. That's what I call my generation. Izods."

"One," Don Cooder said, "you don't have a bomb anymore. And two, if you did, how would it look on television before ninety million people if the camera zoomed in on your neutron bomb and I intoned, 'You are looking at a live neutron device capable of irradiating a three-square-mile metropolitan area with deadly radiation'?"

Sky thought about that. Behind her rose-tinted granny glasses, her brow puckered.

"It would sound scary," she admitted.

"Not just scary, but terrifying. At least a six share terrifying."

"I hadn't thought about that," Sky admitted.

Don Cooder started the car. He had made his

decision. He could always expose the little thief in a follow-up segment.

"Think about it," he said. "Think real hard, because you're going to filch—I mean, steal—enough plutonium to arm that bomb."

"It's tritium. But I don't have the combat casing anymore."

"So? You build another rattrap. My network will pay for it."

"Birdcage" Sky corrected. "And are you sure?"

"Guaranteed. Did you know I'm my own news director?"

"What if the network won't go for it?"

"It's simple. I'll threaten to quit."

"What if they take you up on it?" Sky Bluel asked reasonably. "After all, you are dead last in the ratings."

Don Cooder winced. "You know," he said as the miles of wild blueberry bushes flicked past, "TV news isn't just about ratings. It's about serving the public. About courage. And manhood."

"I'm not a man."

"It's about girlhood too. Hand me that can of hair spray, will you? I think I'm getting a cowlick."

8

Northeast Missouri was getting monotonous, Remo thought sourly.

The road south seemed to go on forever and lead nowhere. He passed only the occasional pickup truck and once a lumbering tractor, moving along the road, which in spots turned to dirt.

On a particularly dusty stretch, Remo had to roll up the windows to keep the stuff out of his lungs.

"If you can get high on dust," he muttered, "those Dirt First!! crazies came to the right place."

From the rear, the Master of Sinanju looked out at the dust billowing by and said nothing. His wizened face was contemplative.

"Chiun," Remo began, "I almost lost you back there, you know."

A tiny twinge crossed the Master of Sinanju's wrinkled countenance. That alone told Remo his words had registered.

"Little Father," he ventured, "it scared me."

Chiun put his nose to the window as if peering more closely at something by the side of the road. Remo's eyes flicked in the same direction, but he could see nothing through the billowing dust and suspected the same was true for Chiun.

Remo pressed on. "You know, we really should

talk about what's eating you. How about a broad hint?"

"Film at eleven," Chiun said firmly.

"Suit yourself," Remo growled, refocusing on his driving.

They found the pickup truck two miles outside the town of Moberly. It stood in a bramble thicket by the roadside.

"This could be a lucky break," Remo said, grinning.

"He who expects to find luck by the side of the road should look to the bottoms of his sandals for unpleasantness," Chiun sniffed.

"Thank you, Charlie Chan," Remo said, pulling onto the soft shoulder of the road.

Remo got out and thrashed through the weeds to the truck.

It was empty. The driver's door stood open. The cab was unoccupied. Going around to the back, Remo found the bed empty too. The tarp was there along with a tangle of loose cables. There were fresh-looking scrapes in the corrugated bed, as if something heavy had been dragged off it.

More important, there were brown handprints.

"Take a look," Remo said as Chiun floated up. "Mystery solved. Only Dirt First!! and five-year-olds leave handprints like these."

Chiun examined the dirty handprints in silence. He went to the other side of the truck. While Remo examined the flatbed more closely, the Master of Sinanju bent to examine the ground.

Aware that Chiun was no longer in his field of vision, Remo said, "Chiun. Where'd you go?"

"I am right here."

"Doing what?"

"Looking at this body."

Remo mouthed the word "body" soundlessly. He reached Chiun's side in three steps.

The body lay sprawled in the thicket. A man. He wore only his underwear—boxer shorts and undershirt. He was tall, and somewhat middle-aged. His ghastly gray face looked up into the sky. His tongue was gray too. It stuck out four inches. His hands were locked around his throat.

"Looks like he choked to death," Remo muttered, closing his wide-open eyes. "Wonder who he is—or was?"

"He is not one of the dirt people," Chiun said.

"Maybe he fell in a creek before he died."

Chiun shook his aged head. "He is too clean," he said, unlocking one stiff hand from its death grip. "Behold, even his fingernails are immaculate."

Remo nodded. His eyes went to the man's face. He couldn't place it, but considering how filthy the Dirt Firsters had been, he couldn't rule the man out as a member, clean fingernails or not. "Maybe he's a reporter," Remo ventured. "Yeah, that's it. This is the reporter Sky Bluel went off with. Those crazies grabbed her, gassed him, and stripped him of his clothes so he couldn't be identified. They probably took his car so they can smuggle the neutron bomb out of state."

Chiun dropped the hand abruptly.

"That is the most absurd concoction I have ever heard," he said stiffly.

"You got a better one?"

"This man is military."

"What makes you say that?" Remo asked, perplexed.

"Examine his forehead. Note the invisible band."

"Invisible . . . ?" Then Remo saw it. A faint red line crossing the corpse's forehead. Remo knelt and twisted the head around. The head turned easily, indicating rigor mortis had not yet set in. The line continued to the back of the man's head as a thin crease in his hair.

"The obvious mark of a military cap," Chiun proclaimed.

"Doesn't make sense. Would Dirt First!! have had an accomplice in the Army or National Guard?"

"Incompetents of a feather," Chiun said carelessly.

"I think you're wrong. This is a headband. That makes him a Dirt Firster, clean fingernails or not." Remo stood up. "Well, whoever he was, he can't help us anymore. Come on, let's see if we can't locate whatever they're transporting the bomb in."

They spent the rest of the afternoon combing the nearby towns and back roads of northeast Missouri. They passed numerous trucks and rambling farm equipment and once even a long white limousine that looked as out-of-place as a Rose Parade float, but no sign of Dirt First!!, the neutron bomb, or Sky Bluel.

The sun had long since set when Remo pulled into a dusty roadside gas station to fill the tank.

While the car was being serviced, Remo found a pay phone.

"Smitty? Remo. I got bad news and worse news."

Smith sighed. "Give me the bad news first."

"We lost Sky Bluel. We can't find Dirt First!! Or the bomb. But we found the truck it was taken away in, not to mention a stray body."

"Body?"

"My words exactly. I hope you're not rubbing off on me, Smitty. You'll find him beside an abandoned pickup outside of Moberly. Don't expect any

ID. He's been stripped. Chiun thinks he's Army or possibly National Guard. I had him pegged for a TV reporter who gave Sky a ride, but now I'm not sure. There were dirty handprints all over the truck."

"Dirt First!!" Smith said tightly.

"Everything points to them," Remo said, watching the sun slip behind a line of haystacks. "Listen, it's night here. I don't think we're going to turn up the girl, the bomb, or the bums. I'd suggest you call out the National Guard, but I've seen them in action. Ditto the Army."

"Since we now know that Dirt First is definitely behind this," Smith said, "I suggest you infiltrate them as soon as possible."

Remo groaned. "I was hoping to avoid that."

"Report any progress as soon as you have made it." Smith disconnected. Remo returned to the car and paid the attendant.

Back on the road, he updated the Master of Sinanju.

"If this is what Smith wishes, then we will do this," Chiun said at last.

"You're serious!" Remo said, in surprise. "You're ready to infiltrate Dirt First!!"

"I did not say I. Obviously *I* cannot."

"Why not?"

"Because no one would ever believe such a ridiculous imposture."

"Okay, I'll bite. What ridiculous imposture?"

"That a Korean would lose his mind so badly as to breathe dirt and wear mud. We are much too civilized."

"So I'm on my own now. Is that it?"

Chiun stroked his wispy beard thoughtfully. "I will accompany you, to rescue you if necessary."

"From what? Succumbing to dirt-induced cancer of the lungs?"

"No, in the event that you find wallowing in filth irresistible. For it was filth that I raised you from, Remo, and I will not lose you to your base white nature."

"The color white," Remo said, watching the road signs, "has absolutely nothing to do with Dirt First!"

9

The national headquarters of Dirt First!! was a shabby Victorian house in San Francisco's Haight-Ashbury district.

"Explain this to me, Remo," the Master of Sinanju said as Remo tooled the rented car through the winding, undulating streets, searching for the address. "If these dirt persons are, as Smith proclaims, terrorists, why is their address to be found in the telephone encyclopedia?"

"It's hard to explain," Remo said distractedly.

"You will try."

"Dirt First!! don't consider themselves terrorists. They think they're saving the environment."

"From whom?"

Remo frowned in thought. "From people, I guess."

"Are people not part of this environment?" Chiun asked, perplexed.

"Not to Dirt First!! To them, a spotted owl has more rights to the wilderness than the people who live and work there. So they vandalize trees by driving spikes into them."

"Are not trees part of the environment?" Chiun asked.

"They are to me."

"Then why would they crucify a poor defenseless tree?"

"Look," Remo said, exasperated, "all I know is what I read in the papers. The point is, they traipse around practically in mudface, so no one knows who they really are. As a group, they take credit for all this squirrely stuff. Individually, they claim it's the work of renegade members they can't control."

"A transparent lie," Chiun said solemnly.

"It works in the courts. They also have good lawyers."

Chiun's tight expression broke in shock. "Those ragamuffins?"

"Disguised ragamuffins. Only their B.O. is on the money. And don't look now, but I think we found Dirt First!! World Headquarters." Remo pointed up the street.

From his seat in back, Chiun peered out the window. The Victorian house looked as if it needed a bath too. Soot grimed its purple-gray sides. The gingerbread dripped with guano. Pigeons roosted in the eaves, adding to the dripping decoration that gave the house its tie-dyed appearance.

"Is this a pest house?" Chiun asked.

"What was your first clue?" Remo asked, pulling over. From the glove compartment he pulled out an assortment of burnt corks and a T-shirt. Like the one he wore, this T-shirt was white. It was streaked with dirt, the result of Remo studiously stomping it into the dirt.

Remo quickly changed shirts. Using the rearview mirror, he rubbed his face, hands, and bare arms with burnt cork.

When he was done, he turned in his seat.

"Think I'll pass?"

"For white?" Chiun asked. And he laughed.

"Think I'll pass?" he repeated. "For white? Heh heh heh. For white? Heh heh heh."

"Har de har har har," Remo growled, but he repressed a smile. Chiun was in a good mood again. Remo hadn't yet figured out why he was in the doghouse, but he wasn't about to spoil the undeclared truce by asking. The memory of losing the Master of Sinanju in the plastique explosion was very fresh. "Ready?"

"I am never prepared to follow a lunatic into a nest of his fellows," Chiun said loftily, "but I will go where you do, for I am curious about these mud people."

"Let me do the talking, okay?"

"No."

Chiun followed Remo up a long flight of guano-spattered concrete steps. He kept his eyes on the eaves all the way to the outer door, dodging two aerial bombs before he reached it.

"I hope it's cleaner inside," Remo said, once they were in the relative safety of the foyer.

There was only one mailbox and one bell. Both read "DIRT FIRST!!" Remo leaned on the bell.

"Who is it?" a voice crackled from the ancient annunciator.

"Potential recruits," Remo said.

"How many of you?"

"Two," said Remo.

"One," said Chiun.

"Which is it?"

"One recruit. One guardian," Chiun said squeakily.

The inner door buzzed. They stepped in, Remo leading.

The smell hit them first. It was a conglomeration of predominantly organic odors. Like the birdhouse of a particularly slovenly zoo.

"Pee-yew!" Remo spat. Chiun lifted a draperylike sleeve to his delicate nose. He breathed through this.

A man greeted them, extending his hand. He was lean, coarse-pored, but well-scrubbed. His equally surprising short hair seemed to explode in all directions. It made Remo wonder if the microwavable hairpiece had been perfected while he was out of the country.

"Barry Kranish," he said affably. "Chief counsel for the Dirt First!! organization. Come in, come in."

"Who's their zookeeper?" Remo asked, gesturing to the collection of bird cages and fish tanks that dominated the polished-mahogany waiting area.

"Gentlemen," Barry Kranish said proudly, "you are looking at the finest collection of endangered species assembled in one building."

Remo gazed around. At his elbow, neon blue and green fish were struggling in an alga-slimed tank. They poked their pouting little mouths up from the waterline, as if hungry.

"Shouldn't you aerate that tank?" Remo suggested.

"Nonsense. This tank replicates their natural environment. Aerators would disturb their natural life cycle."

As Barry Kranish talked, one fish gave up and sank back, upside down. He eventually floated back to the waterline, bobbing like a cork, belly-side-up.

"I think that one died," Remo prompted.

"Is death not part of the natural cycle of eco-reality?"

"Not if you're a fish that can't breathe the water," Remo said, looking to Chiun.

The Master of Sinanju pointed to a bird cage where a brownish-gray owl slept. His eyes were closed. His talons clutched a simple branch balanced between the cage walls.

Chiun clucked loudly. The owl opened balefully orblike yellow eyes. It struggled to shift positions on its perch, but could not move. It flapped its great wings in annoyance.

"Why is that bird wired to his perch?" Chiun inquired.

"I'm glad you asked that." Barry Kranish smiled. "This is the addled woodsy owl, one of our proudest achievements. Dirt First!! saved the last natural habitat of this magnificent creature. Let me show you what makes them special."

Kranish lifted a pair of wire cutters from an end table and, opening the cage door, reached in to snip the bird free.

The owl, beating its wings, flew from the cage. It made a frantic circle of the room. Chiun cast a wary eye ceilingward for dropping guano.

"He'll get tired soon," Barry promised.

"And then what?" Remo asked.

"He'll settle on this perch," Kranish added, taking a gnarled tree branch off the same polished table.

Presently the owl did slow down. Kranish stretched out one arm like a Navy semaphore signalman and the owl settled onto the branch amid a great fluttering of autumnal wings.

It worked its long talons for a moment or two before getting comfortable. And then, closing its eyes, the addled woodsy owl dropped off to sleep.

"This is the inspiring part," Kranish whispered.

As Remo and Chiun watched, the owl began to slip backward, eyes still closed.

The owl realized his problem too late. The round eyes flew open in wise surprise. Then the owl dropped backward off the perch to land on its tufted head with a loud *bonk*!

Remo rushed forward to pick the poor creature off the floor. It was out cold.

"What happened to it?" he wondered, face concerned.

"Oh, they do that all the time," Barry Kranish said airily. "That's the beauty of the addled woodsy owl. Check out the claws."

Remo did. He was no bird expert, but Chiun, leaning over worriedly, proclaimed the problem.

"It does not possess a back claw."

"Precisely," Kranish said with enthusiasm. "Addled owls are mutants. They lack the rear balancing claw, which is why they're always falling off their perches. There are only twenty-eight of them in the whole world, one here. The other twenty-seven are in Oregon, happily falling out of the trees and waking up in confusion. That's why they're called addled."

"This one does not look happy," Chiun pointed out. "Confused, yes. But not happy."

Kranish accepted the limp owl from Remo. "That's because they haven't fully acclimated themselves to their adaptation," he explained. "We think they are the next stage in owl evolution, designed to perch on something other than tree branches. We haven't figured out what yet, but we're committed to preserving them until the owls work it out among themselves."

"Did it ever cross your mind that these might simply be deformed owls?" Remo wondered as, humming, Kranish swiftly rewired the owl to his cage perch. When he was done, it hung upside down.

"That's a very unprogressive attitude you got there," Barry Kranish said disapprovingly.

"Sorry," Remo said contritely. "I really want to join Dirt First!! I'm Remo. This is Chiun. Where are the others?"

"Off doing the good work. I see you've come dressed for war."

"War?" Chiun squeaked.

"We are ecowarriors. The first politically pure vanguard that will sweep the earth clear of all unprogressive elements. When we're done, the global ecosystem will be safe for all life. We will happily coexist, man and monkey, cobra and weasel."

"I'm all for saving the weasels," Remo said with a poker face. "Where do I sign up?"

"In my office. Come, come. But watch your step."

"I see the guano," Remo said.

"I meant the cockroaches. They're rare Venezuelan bull roaches. We had a nest of them shipped in so visitors could appreciate their raw brute beauty."

Remo and Chiun stepped with care. A cockroach that looked like a cross between a very large beetle and a midget armadillo scuttled out of a crevice and went up the side of a fish tank with electrifying speed. As they watched in horror, it reached tiny forelegs into the water and dragged out a squirming fingerling.

Holding it above its waving feelers, it scuttled back for its lair.

Remo and Chiun exchanged glances.

"I will follow," Chiun whispered.

Remo nodded. He went through the door with Kranish.

The Master of Sinanju intercepted the cockroach and crushed it under a white sandal. Pinching the struggling fish between his nails, he returned it to its tank, where it resumed swimming happily.

Wearing a pleased smile, Chiun glided to the closing door.

Inside, the office was paneled in cherrywood. The smell was less rank in here, largely due to the open bay window.

Remo and Chiun gravitated to that window, making a concerted effort to breathe only outside air.

"As I was telling your friend here," Kranish relayed to Chiun, "in order to join Dirt First!! you must sign a release absolving the organization of culpability in any activities you undertake on our behalf."

"Why is that?" Remo wanted to know.

"So if you're arrested or sued, the organization can go on unimpeded," Kranish told him.

"Sounds like you don't place high value on your recruits," Remo muttered, looking at the release form.

Chiun accepted his upside down and made a pretense of reading it. He frowned in mock concentration.

"Listen," Kranish said, "Dirt First is about the environment. It is not about people. People are the disease, not the cure. If you join us, you must sublimate your identity to the group ethos."

Remo looked blank. "Ethos?"

"In Dirt We Trust!" Barry Kranish said sternly.

"In dirt . . . ?"

"Surely you understand dirt. You're smeared with it. Are you ready to undertake the initiation?"

"What's it involve?" Remo asked suspiciously.

"Oh, not much. You take a little swim and commune with a few of nature's rare creatures. After that you imbibe a natural beverage that purges the system."

"Doesn't sound too bad," Remo said slowly.

"Spoken like a gullible white," Chiun hissed.

"What'd he say?" Barry Kranish asked.

"He said, 'Let's get it over with.' "

"Excellent. Come this way, please."

Barry Kranish led them back out to the reception area, where a bull cockroach was silently fishing at another tank.

Chiun brushed it in passing. It plopped into the water, where its weight carried it to the gravel bottom. The hungry fish began to bite off its waving legs.

Passing through a paneled door, they descended a flight of steps to a cool basement area lit by fluorescent lights set in long ceiling tubes. The lights were reflected in a long Olympic-size indoor pool. The water reflections shimmied and shook at the vibrations of their approach. Or Barry Kranish's approach, inasmuch as Remo and Chiun sent out no more vibration than a legless bull cockroach.

Remo looked onto the pool. It was not the cleanest water he had ever seen. At the other end, he detected sinuous needlelike shapes swimming in languorous circles.

"Cockroaches?" Remo asked doubtfully.

"No, catfish. A rare South American variety, I might add."

Remo visibly relaxed. "So what do I do?"

"First, you get naked."

"I am not getting naked," Remo said firmly.

"It's the rules. No naked, no membership."

"I am not getting naked," Remo repeated.

"He is only saying that because he is ashamed to reveal that he is hung like a duck," Chiun said archly.

Remo shot the Master of Sinanju an ugly look. "I'll get naked," he relented.

"And I will turn my back," Chiun said, quickly

suiting action to words. Unseen, he grinned broadly. American slang had its uses.

Stripping off his T-shirt, Remo stepped out of his shoes.

"What do I do after I'm undressed?" he asked, reaching for his belt.

Barry Kranish smiled benevolently. "Simple. You step into the pool, wade to the other end, and come back. I'll give you a little libation and you're officially a member of Dirt First!!"

"Okay," Remo said, dropping his pants. Leaving his underwear at poolside, he stepped into the water, setting himself for what he expected would be a cold and clammy experience.

To his surprise, the water was tropically warm. He slipped in up to his waist and started for the far end of the pool. The vibrations of his approach sent waves that disturbed the catfish at the other end. They ceased their circular swimming activity, paused, and then, as if homing in on a school of fishy mates, made a concerted rush toward Remo.

"This isn't so bad," Remo said. "Here, fishy, fishy."

The fish came at him like speedy brown needles. They seemed unafraid. Probably trained, he thought. Remo advanced to meet them.

The water rose up to his lower ribs. Then it sloshed around his armpits. It felt good, especially on his cork-dusted arms. Remo lost sight of the catfish. But as they swam by, their tiny bodies disturbed the water slightly, just enough to tickle the cilialike hairs on his legs, his natural warning antennae.

"They tickle," Remo said, smiling tentatively.

His expression froze. "Hey!" he said. Then, "What the dingdong hell are they doing!" in a louder voice.

"Just relax," Barry Kranish called. "They won't hurt you. They're only doing what comes naturally."

Remo didn't hear Barry Kranish's words of reassurance. He executed a sudden back flip. It lifted him straight up into the air. He landed barefoot and dripping on the edge of the pool, where he started slapping at his legs. His fingers came away with bright spots of blood. His blood. He felt one slick slimy shape on his inner thigh and ripped it free. He threw it back into the water.

Fists clenched, he advanced on Barry Kranish.

"What the hell were those things?" Remo thundered.

Backing away from the venomous glare in Remo's dark eyes, Barry Kranish sputtered, "Catfish. Just South American catfish. *Genus Vandellia*. They're called *candiru*."

"Never heard of them."

"They're an endangered species. Really. The Jivaro Indians of the Amazon have been trying to exterminate them for years."

"Gee, I wonder why," Remo said, grabbing Kranish by one quaking pinstriped shoulder.

"They wouldn't have hurt you," Kranish protested. "They wouldn't have taken very much blood. You see, only one or two could enter you at one time."

"Enter? Enter where?"

"Yes," Chiun chimed in, turning around. "What do you mean by enter my son?" Then, seeing Remo's glistening backside, Chiun averted his eyes. One long-nailed hand went up to his eyes. He peered through the chinks between his bony fingers.

"Those are *candiru*," Kranish said nervously. "They're wonderfully specialized creatures. They slip into bodily orifices, where they erect spines to anchor themselves to their host."

"They what!" Remo said, face darkening.

"Then they, uh, drink blood. But only a little," he added hastily. "They're quite small, after all. Just babies. Cute little babies."

"*Vampire* babies," Chiun chimed in.

"Then what?" Remo prompted.

Barry Kranish swallowed. "Well, if they're not removed, they could suck a man dry in a matter of days, but there's a wonderfully wholesome natural way of purging them from the host. It's the libation I told you about." He grabbed an old milk bottle from a nearby cobwebbed shelf. It was filled with a pulpy liquid that was the exact color of pureed apricots.

"See?" he said, holding it up to Remo's face. "Jagua juice." His hands shook. Yellowish pulp dribbled from the open bottle. "One drink of this and any *candiru* would have expelled itself in a matter of thirty-six hours. No harm done. A blood test would have taken more serum."

Remo looked into Barry Kranish's fear-haunted eyes.

"I've changed my mind," he said at last.

"About joining?"

"No," Remo said harshly. "About screwing around with you Dirt First dirtbags." Remo pushed Barry Kranish up against the wall.

"Come again?"

"No, you go ahead," Remo said, swiping the bottle from his jittery hands.

"Go?" Kranish's eyes went to the pool. They widened with worry. "You don't mean . . . ?"

"Time to get reinitiated," Remo sang.

Lifting the man bodily, Remo plunged him, pinstriped suit and all, into the pool. The aimlessly swarming *candiru* took instant notice. From all directions, they arrowed after him.

"No, no, I've already done this!" Kranish moaned, splashing frantically. "Once is enough!"

Struggling to the edge of the pool, Barry Kranish tried to lever himself to safety. Remo's bare feet, feeling more like diver's lead boots than flesh and bone, were there to discourage him. Remo stamped on Kranish's fingers. Kranish retreated, the spiny catfish following him like free-swimming magnets.

"What is this stuff?" Remo asked, hefting the bottle of yellowish juice. "Baby poop?"

"Be . . . be careful!" Kranish cried. "Don't drop it!"

"Come to think of it," Remo said, tossing the bottle to his other hand, "this glass is kinda slick." He made a pretense of nearly dropping it to the tiled floor.

"Please," Barry Kranish pleaded, splashing the water all around him. "I'll do anything." He might have been surrounded by ferocious goblin sharks instead of the minnowlike *candiru*, for all the terror that seized his thin face.

"Talk fast," Remo suggested.

"About what?"

"The neutron bomb. Which one of your lunatics has it?"

"I have no idea what you're talking about. Truly."

"The La Plomo incident," Remo suggested. "Your people were there, mucking up the tragedy worse than it was."

"I know nothing about that. Members are on their own recognizance in matters of ecotage."

"What?"

"Ecotage!" Kranish said, doing a four-limbed

splash. "It's our term for ecological sabotage. Also known as monkey-wrenching."

"I thought you guys were trying to save the environment, not sabotage it."

"We are! We are! Really! We just liked the sound of ecotage—it's so dramatic. What do you want from me?"

"A neutron bomb was brought to the gas site to make a statement," Remo explained. "It was stolen. We think your people have it."

"I swear to you. If any of my people had a neutron bomb, they would have brought it to my attention. For legal advice."

"Your people check in from La Plomo yet?"

"Yes. They called. They said something about Palm Springs. I think they're planning a sit-in at the Condome site."

"Did you say condo or condom?" Remo asked.

"Neither. Condome. It's a construction project. I'm surprised you never heard of it. It was on the cover of last month's *Mother Jones*."

"What are they up to?"

"I don't know and I didn't ask. But they didn't sound happy. If they had a neutron bomb, I would know about it."

Remo turned to Chiun. "What do you think, Little Father?"

"He is telling the truth, Remo," Chiun said through shielded eyes. "Now, put on your clothes. You are embarrassing me, parading around like that."

Remo jerked a thumb at the splashing lawyer. "What about this idiot?"

"He no longer matters."

"But he tried to feed me to the fish. Literally."

"*Candiru*," Kranish bleated, tears streaming from his eyes. "Innocent endangered baby *candiru*."

Remo stepped back from the pool.

Barry Kranish stumbled up, eyes blazing with fear. He stood on the edge of the pool, not sure which was more critical—drinking his so-called libation or getting out of his clothes in order to examine his bodily orifices for spiny intruders.

He ultimately decided to do both.

Remo and Chiun left him squirming at poolside, half in and half out of his clothes, chugalugging viscous jagua juice in sobbing gulps.

10

If a human being could truly be called a human chameleon, Dr. Harold W. Smith was a perfect specimen. He possessed the unique ability to blend into any social situation. Especially if the background was a bland, neutral gray.

Smith wore his gray three-piece suit like a badge of uniformity. His crisp hair was a lighter shade of gray, as were his weak eyes. Even his skin possessed a grayish tinge. Only his tie—a striped Dartmouth school tie—displayed any color. If Dr. Smith possessed a soul—and there was some doubt about this—no doubt it would have been gray, as well.

If anything, Dr. Smith resembled a stuffy university professor, perhaps the chairman of the Social Science Department of a rustic New England college. The nameplate on his door said "Dr. Harold W. Smith, Director." Only three other persons knew that Folcroft Sanitarium in Rye, New York, was cover for CURE and that Smith was its director too.

His mouth was a prim line in his studious gray face as he bent over his computer terminal, which, at the touch of a button, could be sent sinking back into a concealed well in his desk. The prim line deepened into a worried frown.

Luminous green lines of text scrolled up his screen—data feeds processed by the bank of powerful computers that huddled two floors below his Spartan office overlooking Long Island Sound.

While Remo and Chiun pursued their end of the La Plomo investigation, Smith had been following the trail of the Lewisite gas that had been loosed on the defenseless Missouri town. After Remo had reported his discovery of the empty gas canisters, Smith had dutifully informed the President of the United States, his direct superior.

The President had ordered the gas canisters removed to an FBI lab for analysis. The preliminary results, moving through the phone lines to the White House and designated "Eyes Only of the President," had been intercepted by Smith's computers. Their ability to reach out and capture free-flowing data was unrivaled.

The FBI report was succinct. Smith's computers had automatically compressed them into an easy-to-read summary. The gist was that the poison gas was U.S. Army war surplus.

With the post-cold-war build-down, Army stockpiles were ending up in some strange places. These gas canisters had been mislabled as pesticide and sold through a General Accounting Office auction, whose proceeds went to lowering the national debt.

"My God!" Smith gasped as the cold facts sank in.

The red phone at Smith's right hand suddenly rang. An ordinary standard desk model except for lack of a dial, it was a dedicated line to the White House.

Smith lifted it to his ear.

"Yes, Mr. President?" he asked, adjusting his rimless glasses.

"Smith," said the nasal voice of the President of

the United States, "I've just received a report on that poison-gas thing. You'll never believe this. It was—"

"Sold by the GAO as pesticide," Smith supplied dryly.

The President gasped. "That's right. How'd you know?"

Because he did not wish the President of the United States to know that his own phones were subject to CURE interception, Smith said, "I have my own sources," and changed the subject. "I understand there is no ID on the final purchaser."

"No. It was a cash transaction. The FBI's hit a dead end."

"Not necessarily. A good FBI sketch of the buyer may give us something to pursue."

"I'll have them get right on it," the President said quickly.

"Do not bother," Smith said crisply. "I will handle that on this end."

"Very well. How are your people doing with that neutron-bomb insanity?"

"It's too early to tell," Smith said evasively.

"Well, I think you were right—exactly right—to put them on that detail," the President confided. "We can't have college students building nuclear devices. What with the crazy college kids these days, there's no telling what might happen. No telling."

"There's more to it than that," Smith said. "I have reason to believe that Dirt First!! was behind the gas attack."

"I'll have the FBI sweep the whole lot of them up. Criticize my environmental record, will they? I'll show 'em."

"No," Smith said flatly. "At the moment, our evidence is circumstantial. But their appearance on the La Plomo scene smacks of exactly the kind of publicity stunt they're known to indulge in."

"My God!" the President said hoarsely. "Is that what you think this is all about—a publicity stunt?"

"It is a theory. They were badly discredited last year when two of their members were injured in a bombing that turned out to have been the work of other members of the group who advocate using violence to protect the environment. They need to have their credibility restored. I am assuming Dirt First!! obtained the Lewisite, deployed it, and then showed up to reap the publicity benefit of an apparent chemical-storage accident."

"The girl who built the bomb. You think she's connected with these loonies?"

"Unknown," Smith admitted. "I suspect otherwise. The La Plomo event has drawn a great number of protest groups. She may have been just another of those. But her appearance was unfortunate. My best estimate is that Dirt First!! exhausted their entire gas supply on La Plomo. The neutron bomb unfortunately represents a clear substitute for poison gas."

"You think they intend to use it?"

"We have to assume the worst-case scenario. You see, Mr. President, it all ties together."

"Except for one thing."

"And that is?"

"If these people are so committed to the environment, why the hell are they going around doing these crazy things? They say they want to save the redwoods, then drive spikes into them as if they're leafy vampires. They claim their goal is to preserve the environment for future generations, but they don't seem to give a hang about the generation trying to make a living today. Can you explain any of that to me?"

"No, I cannot," Smith said crisply. "I will get back to you when I have progress to report on either front."

"Thank you, Dr. Smith," said the President. "God bless."

Smith returned to his computer and began to input commands that would be routed to the FBI as if coming from the Department of Justice.

Within twenty minutes an FBI forensic sketch artist was parked at a drawing board, an official report tacked to one corner and an open line to a GAO auctioneer in hand. Wondering what was so important, he developed a charcoal sketch of the person described to him.

This image was soon faxed to FBI branches nationwide.

In Rye, New York, Smith watched his own copy of the FBI sketch come off his machine.

The man looked to be between forty and fifty years old, with short hair and what looked to be an old hippie-style headband circling his forehead. Even the hair over his ears stuck out a little under the headband's pressure.

The man did not otherwise look like a typical headband wearer, so Smith read over the artist's remarks in the left-hand margin.

There it was noted that the distinct line was not a headband, but a pressure impression. The artist speculated it was created by a habitually worn headband or possibly a hat.

Otherwise, the man was undistinguished.

"Dirt First!!" Smith said softly, nodding to himself. He dropped the sheet of fax paper into an old-fashioned wire basket so that it settled into place with mathematical precision.

Smith returned to his computer, wrists resting on the edge of the keyboard. He got down to work, after which not even his shoulders moved. If the wall behind him had been gray, he would have been virtually invisible.

In a larger sense, he was.

11

Fabrique Foirade was determined to save the defenseless California desert scorpion.

After his humiliation in La Plomo—where he was all but ignored by the press because of an under-thirty gloryhound with a neutron bomb, and thwarted by other reactionary elements—he had led his troops away.

"Where are we going, Fab?" they had asked.

"Underground," he replied, glowering his frustration.

"But we are underground. We're in the great tradition of Jerry Rubin and Abbie Hoffman, may they rest in peace."

"Jerry's not dead," someone whispered.

"He's worse than dead," Fabrique snapped. "He's a stockbroker. And I know we're underground. We're going deeper than underground. We're going subterranean."

By subterranean, the shock troops of Dirt First!! discovered that a Ramada Inn in Kirkland, Missouri, was meant. They checked in by MasterCard.

They would have used paper money, but they had read that paper was made from wood pulp, which came from trees. It was news to them, but the thought of contributing to the felling of one proud pine by trafficking in folding money was too much for them to bear. After a soul-searching argument, they went with the hated nonbiodegradable plastic tool of capitalism. But only after Fabrique had pointed out that if paper money was out, so were paper checks.

"We're morally excused from paying the MasterCard bill," he concluded. "So there."

At the Ramada, they subjected themselves to hot showers. Some members, long underground, had to be forcibly pushed into the stalls and held down as the sacred soil was drummed from their skins by despised filtered water.

When it was over, they were clean. And unrecognizable.

"Fabrique, is that you?"

"I'm not sure. I don't smell like myself. Joyce?"

"This is amazing. You're a girl. I thought you were a guy!"

Acquaintances renewed, they squatted in an Indian circle to plot strategy.

"We failed," a woman moaned. "None of the cameras were pointed at us." Her greenish teeth were bared in disgust.

"There are other cameras," Fabrique said reassuringly. "Other events. La Plomo ultimately doesn't matter because no trees died, only farmers, and the only animals that were affected were cows. We're not committed to saving the cows."

"But cows are good," someone pointed out. "I used to drink milk before I went vegetarian."

"The world is full of cows," Fabrique said wisely. "We've gotta save the unprotected species first. We'll save the cows later. If they need it."

"But what unprotected species? We've saved most of the important ones. Even those far out addled owls."

"We haven't saved the desert scorpion."

Squatting on the rug, the members of Dirt First!! exchanged quizzical glances. There were more than a few double takes at the many unfamiliar scrubbed faces.

"Is it endangered?" Fabrique was asked.

"Not yet. But soon it will be. Because of one man."

"What man?"

"The grinning pig we saw at the event."

Fabrique flipped a business card into the center of the powwow circle. It landed with a heavy plop.

Someone picked it up, curious.

"Oh, this is one of those condom cards that goofy guy was handing out. Condominia? Is that plural for 'condoms'? I thought 'condoms' was plural for 'condoms'."

" 'Condominia' is plural for 'condominiums,' " Fabrique said gravely. "And condos are the greatest threat to the desert ecosystem since water."

A chorus of gasps raced around the room. Everyone knew what a terrible threat to the natural order water was. Their hair was still wet.

"And by far," Fabrique continued, his voice ringing with indignation, "the most important species to walk the desert is the poor defenseless scorpion. Until this man, this Swindell, came along. I read about him. He's displaced the scorpion population for his stupid Condome complex. And to serve who? Mere people. The scorpion is rightful lord and master of the desert, and we're gonna put him back on his sandy throne!"

Fabrique Foirade raised a righteous fist.

"I move that Dirt First!! declare war on this Swindell defiler person," he shouted.

"I second that!"

The motion passed unanimously. But then, they always did.

"Then it's settled," Fabrique Foirade said, standing up. "We go to California, to the high desert, to rescue the oppressed scorpion! Kilmer, you make the plane reservations. Standby, of course. Joyce, you alert the media. Karen, you have charge of the spikes."

"But, Fab, honey. What'll we need spikes for? We're going to the desert, where there aren't any trees."

That stopped Fabrique Foirade a moment. His long pause held the others raptly. It meant he was thinking—always an event.

"But they do have cacti," he shouted at last. "We'll spike the cacti! If that defiler left any standing."

Through the miracle of nonbiodegradable plastic, the vanguard of Dirt First!! ecowarriors found themselves, a mere seven hours later, in Los Angeles, where they put in a call to their legal representative, Barry Kranish. Collect.

"Barry, babe," Fabrique said, "you'll never guess, man. We're on the most right-on crusade."

"Don't tell me," Barry Kranish said sharply.

"Don't you want to hear how the La Plomo thing went?"

"I know how it went. The six-o'clock news is full of that retro-sixties girl with the neutron bomb. I think I recognized you in the background, spiking a tree, though. Nice going."

"What we got now is better than dead farmers. Bigger than neutron bombs. Scorpions! We're going to stop that cruel Condome project they're building out by Palm Springs."

"I don't want to hear it," Kranish said hastily.

"Just try not to get arrested. Now that we're into plastic, I won't be able to bail you out like before. Most judges don't take plastic."

"And Dirt First!! doesn't take any shit off the Man!" crowed Fabrique Foirade. "See you on the eleven-o'clock news!"

But before Fabrique Foirade could get on the eleven-o'clock news he first had to get out into the desert. Plastic got him from Los Angeles by small plane to Palm Springs Municipal Airport and the forbidding edge of the desert.

After that, it became tricky. To ride on the plastic magic carpet required that there be someone to honor it. Unfortunately, there was no one in Palm Springs from whom they could buy, beg, or borrow a car.

"Look, all we wanna do in drive out into the desert," Fabrique explained to the Sure Lease rental agent.

The agent was firm. "Sorry, we don't accept MasterCard. American Express, sure. Visa, definitely. Cash, absolutely. MasterCard, no."

Fabrique pounded the countertop. "But we gotta get out there. It's an ecoemergency. We're here to save the scorpion."

"I'm a Beatles fan myself," the rental agent said, turning aside and pretending to shuffle some important paperwork in the hope the dozen scruffy hippies would leave his office.

But they didn't leave. They huddled in a corner speaking in low, increasingly violent tones. They were arguing.

The rental agent stationed himself closer to overhear, but could not. It was very strange, he thought, the way they would argue with such vehemence without making any intelligible words.

Finally the argument subsided and the leader—he was taller than the rest and wilder of eye—returned to the counter.

"Are you sure you don't want to save the scorpion?" he asked in a very calm voice.

"Not my job," the rental agent returned coolly.

"Too bad," said the wild-eyed man. He reached out and took him by the collar.

"Hey!" said the rental agent as he was dragged across the counter to the other side. He was so surprised that he didn't fight back. Renters had never gotten violent with him before, not here in the golfing capital of the world.

Very quickly he was sorry he hadn't fought back, because he was slammed to the floor and the wild-eyed guy was pulling a mallet from his knapsack.

"Okay, okay," the agent said excitedly. "Take a car. Don't hit me."

"I'm not going to hit you," Wild-Eyes said in a steady voice as the others grabbed his arms and legs. The rest placed heavy metal objects on his throat, chest, and stomach.

"What are those?" he asked uncomfortably.

"Spikes."

It was the last word he ever heard, because the mallet drove down in a sweeping overhand blow, pushing the cold steel into his throat. He died instantly. But to be sure, the hammerer drove the other two spikes into his chest and stomach.

His dead hands dropped to the parquet floor.

When he got to the Condome site, hours later, Fabrique Foirade's first reaction was one of disappointment.

"There's no fence," he complained. "How are we gonna block the heavy equipment from entering if there's no fence?"

"There isn't even any heavy equipment," Joyce spat.

Fabrique Foirade took in the gleaming Condome complex with a grim expression.

The great Plexiglas bubble had been finished. They could see the Spanish-colonial penthouse inside. All around the wide-open work area, construction workmen in yellow hard hats lugged prefabricated walls and other objects through an open door in the bubble. It resembled a colossal airlock.

As they watched, one lone worker, stooping to pick up a discarded drill, gave an ear-splitting shriek. He dropped the tool.

"Scorpion!" he yelled. He started stomping the ground with his heavy construction boots. "Damn you!"

"He's butchering that poor bug!" Fabrique hissed. "Doesn't he know he should love all of nature's creatures?"

"Let's show him how," Fabrique said menacingly.

Shouting, Dirt First!! poured from their sheltering dune.

The construction worker who had had the misfortune to disturb a scorpion hiding in the shade of his power drill was sick of scorpions. Truth to tell, Edward Coyne was sick of the Condome project with its never-ending problems. So he was happy to have something to take his troubles out on. Even if it was a scorpion.

He stomped it hard. The tail curled up as if suddenly sucked dry. He stomped its head. He thought that did it, but the damned thing was still moving. It tried to scuttle away.

"Got you now, you devil," Ed said bitingly, lifting a heavy boot to deliver the coup de grace.

The coup de grace was never delivered because

out of the desert came a horde of . . . Ed Coyne didn't know what the hell they were. They looked like atomic-blast victims with their dusty skin, matted hair, and wild red-rimmed eyes.

Whatever they were, they were shouting, Dirt First!! Dirt First!!"

"Dirt?" he muttered. "We're in the desert."

Then they were all over him.

Ed Coyne was a big man, six-five and 225 pounds, with case-hardened hands like wooden mauls. He laid the first wave out cold. After that, he had a rougher time of it. They attacked him with the rounded ends of railroad spikes, banging on his hard hat with a vengeance and howling, "Spike him! Spike him!"

One lifted a mallet behind a spike, coming toward him looking like a crazed version of *Dracula*'s Van Helsing.

That was enough for Ed Coyne. Struggling with the ones who were straining to pull him to the ground, he reached down for the electric drill. He hoped no one had kicked the cord loose from the generator plug.

No one had. His fingers closed around the trigger, and as he squeezed, he heard the reassuring high-pitched whine of the drill bit.

Ed brought it up like a pistol and waved it in the face of his attacker.

"Who's got cavities that need work?" he taunted. "The dentist is in!"

That did the trick. They changed their minds about spiking him. In fact, they changed their minds about everything.

"Retreat! Retreat!" the one with the mallet and spike shouted.

They slunk back into the desert. One stopped to gently gather up the wounded scorpion with two tender hands. He was stung for his pains. Howling, he dropped the insect and followed the others, crying that he loved the scorpion. Why couldn't it love him back?

The commotion brought the rest of the crew running from the Condome, where they were stowing tools for the night.

"Who the hell were they?" Ed was asked.

"I don't know. They kept yelling 'Dirt First!' Mean anything to you?"

"Oh, hell, it's those ecocrazies. You know, the ones who are forever trying to save every halt-and-lame subspecies of useless pest in the forest."

"But we're in the desert."

"I guess the forest got too hot for them," Ed Coyne remarked, gathering up his drill and cord. "Come on, we'd better tell Mr. Swindell. He's gonna love this."

12

Connors "Con" Swindell was not having a good day.

In truth, he wasn't having a good year. The way things were going, he was well on his way to having a terrible decade.

It had all been so different back in the seventies and eighties, when he had been one of the giants in condomania.

As if it were yesterday, Con Swindell remembered those halcyon days. Especially the forever-golden moment the cabalistic word "condominium" had been whispered in his ear.

"Condoleum?" he had sputtered, perplexed.

"No, condominium."

"Condolonium," Swindell repeated, blinking.

It had been a real-estate conference in Phoenix. The man who whispered in his ear added, "It's the greatest thing to hit real estate since the thirty-year fixed-rate mortgage."

"Condomonium?" Con said, still struggling with the unfamiliar word.

"Condominiums," Morgan Mullaney repeated, a slight edge creeping into his usually smooth salesman's voice. He was in the high end of the residential market. Strictly penthouses and mansions. Nothing less than six-figure transactions.

"Why don't we just call them cons—just to get through the conversation?" Swindell had suggested, wondering if this guy was trying to snooker him somehow.

"How about condos?" Mullaney suggested. " 'Cons' sounds a little shady. No offense, you understand."

"None taken," said Connors Swindell, who had made a lateral career slide from used cars into real estate. He happened to have been sucked into buying some worthless Florida land back in the early sixties. Then Disney World had been hatched and Connors cashed in his worthless land for big bucks. He got out of used cars and traded up to fine homes. He had been trading up ever since, feeding the voracious public appetite for the American dream's ultimate aspiration, a home of one's own.

"So," he asked on that long-ago day, "what exactly are condos?"

Connors Swindell found himself being led to a display booth. There was a scale model of a Spanish-style apartment house tended by a busty blond. He had trouble keeping his eyes on the model.

"Nice," he said. "But I'm in private homes. Rentals are a pain. I like to sell 'em and walk away. Let the banks worry about whether the suckers are good for the mortgage."

"This, my friend, is no mere apartment house."

"Looks like one. Bigger than some, smaller than most. So what?"

"What would you say if I told you that this baby will generate more income than a comparable apartment house would if you rented it out for fifty years straight?"

"Where you plan on building it—Beverly Hills?"

"Burbank."

"Burbank! You're dreaming!"

"No, I'm developing. I'm in development now, Con. Condominium development."

"There's that word again," Swindell mumbled, staring at the apartment-house model. "How's it work?"

"Very simply. Inside and out, it looks just like a common apartment house. But you *don't* rent out the units."

Swindell licked his teeth. "How do you make money, then?"

"You *sell* them."

"Sell apartments?"

"No, sell condos," Mullaney said, detaching the plastic-stucco facade from the model building.

Swindell leaned over to peer inside. He saw tiny apartments containing tiny people seated on tiny furniture.

"I don't get it," he remarked. "Looks like an ordinary apartment to me."

"Look, why do people rent?"

" 'Cause they can't afford to buy. Everyone knows that."

"Exactly. So with condos they buy their apartments."

"No one in their right fucking mind would buy a fucking apartment," Swindell said indignantly, deciding his colleague was pulling his chain. "Don't kid a kidder. No one is that crazy."

"You're right, Con, ol' buddy. No one would buy an apartment. What would they be buying? The inner walls and floor? The cube of air inside those walls? No way, right? But if you call it a condominium, folks will line right up. And you know why?"

"No, why?"

"Because there are so damn many young couples coming up now that there won't be houses enough for all of them. People with fine jobs and plenty of down payment rattling around in their savings accounts. But no houses. You've heard of the baby boom?"

"Yeah. I was one of the first to drop down the chute, back in forty-six. My old man knocked up my old lady as soon as he got back from Guam. Smartest thing he ever did, if I do say so myself."

"Well, there's plenty more where you came from. And they've all got an itch to own. Well, I got the solution right here."

Swindell frowned. "Never work. Not in a million years. You couldn't build these things cheap enough. Look at it, what is it? Stucco facing over concrete butresses? Too expensive. Never work."

"They will if you price them a third higher than comparable rental units," Morgan Mullaney said smugly.

"Higher! You nuts?"

"Hey, if you rent, you're throwing your money away. But if you buy . . ."

A tiny green gleam came into Connors Swindell's eyes then.

He left the conference early and sold off his entire residential inventory, using the proceeds to float construction loans.

Within a year he was building condo apartments from San Diego to Sacramento. And when he ran out of cheap land, he sank his profits into existing apartment houses and converted those into condos. Single-handedly, Connors Swindell initiated the move into condo conversion, which threw old people out of affordable apartments and into despair, but made him too rich to care.

From a California-based corporation, Swindell Properties Incorporated swept the nation like a forest fire. It built condos, condexes, and co-ops.

Warehouses fell before him. Apartment houses were exalted by his alchemic touch. By the time he was through, he was razing perfectly healthy schools, churches, fire stations, amusement parks, and even entire tracts of single-family houses, replacing them with sprawling condominium town houses.

Connors Swindell was on a roll unprecedented in real-estate history. He grew powerful, wealthy, virtually omnipotent. Bankers fought one another for his business. He could float a loan on nothing more than a toothy grin and the collateral in his wallet.

As the solid 1970's faded into the expansive eighties, Connors Swindell left them all in the dust, including Morgan Mullaney, the man who had first spoken that magic word.

The secret of his success was simple. Swindell Properties didn't build better condominiums. Nor affordable ones.

Swindell built pronounceable condominiums.

"Call 'em condos," he lectured his growing sales force. "No one's gonna buy what they can't spell." And he was right.

Once "condo" became a household word, he was unstoppable.

Then came the stock-market crash of 1987.

"I can ride this out," Swindell had crowed, and kept on building. So a few yuppies had bitten the big one. The market was going to come roaring back. And it did.

What didn't come roaring back were the yuppies and the banks. Credit dried up. In a way, he was a victim of his own success. Everybody had plunged into the condo game. Competition was fierce. But demand dwindled. Loans stopped coming. Interest piled up. Defaults followed. The entire nation had been overbuilt. Somehow.

Almost overnight, it seemed, Connors Swindell went from being the darling of the real-estate industry to a desperate man presiding over a sprawling chain of halted construction projects, nervous lenders, and mounting debt.

"Somebody explain this to me," Swindell had moaned at a real-estate conference twenty years later. This one in Lake Tahoe.

No one could. They were all going around wearing the same dazed and vaguely frightened looks on their gloomy faces. Even the ones who had stayed in family homes. Prices there had shot through the roof during the real-estate-as-an-investment mania. Even house prices were flat now. No one could remember it being this bad. "Not since the Great Depression," they lamented.

After the fourth person had repeated that refrain, Connors Swindell retreated to the men's room to vomit or take a hit of coke. Possibly both.

He was unzipping his fly when he became aware of a well-dressed man standing before the next urinal. Lean and elegant, he had Princeton written all over him.

Connors Swindell calculated his age to be roughly eighty.

"Say, old-timer," he said over the sound of his liquid lunch rushing from his body, "everybody says it ain't been like this since the thirties. You lived through those times. Can you tell me what the future will bring? Are condos defunct?"

"You want to know why everything flattened out?" the old man asked.

"Sure."

"Well, finish up what you're doing and I'll show you."

Swindell hastily squeezed himself dry and followed the man over to the row of sinks. Instead of washing his hands, the man turned and said, "Got a quarter?"

"Barely," Connors grunted, fishing into his pockets. He handed the old duffer a quarter. The man turned around and put it into the coin slot of a wall-mounted vending machine. He turned the lever and the machine went *ching-chuck!* Something flat slid down into a slot.

The old man held it up to the weak light.

Swindell saw it was a foil-wrapped package.

"Are you deaf? This here's a fucking condom. Not a condo."

"What are these used for, my friend?"

"If you don't know by now, the information ain't gonna do you much good," Swindell said flatly.

"This little number protects against unwanted offspring."

"You ain't making a whole bushel of sense."

"Think back. When did these items become popular again?"

"Oh, about four, five years ago, when that AIDS thing started getting out of hand."

"Exactly. Before that, you couldn't get most young fellas to pull one of these on if it came packaged with Jean Harlow. She was an actress. Made Madonna look like Stan Laurel in drag. He was an actor. Anyway, birth control was a thing the women got saddled with, with their pills and diaphragms and the like. But come AIDS, and it was every man for himself. So to speak."

"I still don't follow."

"You got into this business, when? The sixties? Seventies?"

"Late sixties," Swindell admitted, eyeing the condom. "Why?"

"You, my friend rode the baby boom to success."

"Don't I know it!" Swindell said fervently.

"Well, the baby boom just bottomed out. And there ain't no baby boomlet coming along to save your butt. And you can thank that little device you got in your hands for that."

Connors Swindell regarded the foil package as if seeing it for the first time. And the truth fell on him like a rain of anvils.

"These fucking things are gonna ruin the business!"

"Now you know," said the old man, smiling gently. He tossed him the foil packet. Swindell caught it. "Keep it. You paid for it. And I think you're gonna keep paying for it."

That had been in 1990. The year Connors Swindell got his first inkling he was in for a rough decade.

But he was a fighter. And a schemer. He wasn't about to go down the tubes with the others. He would find a way to come back.

And he was doing just that. Sure, the road was rocky. But he was starting a comeback. Step one was to go back to basics. Real houses. Prices were already falling. They'd fall some more. Like stocks. He'd just have to buy cheap and hang on until real estate bounced back.

Meanwhile, Connors Swindell looked around for the cheapest land he could find. He found it practically in his own backyard. The California desert.

He traded an entire condo park for a hundred square miles of Indian-reservation desert less than five miles from his Palm Springs office. Arid, endless, and commercially worthless. The Indians who had consummated the deal must have thought they were getting payback for the Manhattan deal.

What they didn't know was that Swindell's condos had been built from substandard materials over a toxic-waste landfill.

One day Connors Swindell took a young loan

officer out to his desert in a rented jeep. The Little San Bernardino Mountains reared up over the desert-penetrating Colorado River Aqueduct.

"Nobody builds in the desert," the loan officer was saying. He was a green, wet-behind-the-ears kid. Probably a trainee. That was how little the banks thought of Swindell Properties in 1990.

"I remember a young realtor once saying that no one would pay good money for an apartment," Swindell pointed out. "Want a drink?" he added, offering a thermos capped by a clear plastic cup.

"What is it?" the loan officer asked suspiciously.

"Gatorade. It'll replace the minerals you're sweating away."

The loan officer accepted the thermos, and uncapping it, poured green liquid into the clear cup. He drank it down greedily.

"Don't lose the cap. It's important," Swindell said.

"I beg your pardon?"

"Trust me."

The Gatorade was nearly gone when they reached the spot.

"Here it is," Swindell said proudly.

"How can you tell?" asked the loan officer, looking around unhappily. "There's nothing but sand in all directions."

"My patch has scorpions. Watch your feet."

Connors Swindell led the young loan officer in his banker's gray to a gently undulating expanse of sand. Swindell carried the thermos with the plastic lid.

"You are standing on the exact site of the world's first Condome," he announced suddenly, stamping the ground.

"Did you say condom?" the loan officer said, vaguely offended.

"Dome. Con*dome*," Swindell repeated, experiencing a momentary flash of *déjà vu*. "Get it right. Condome. I'm gonna sink the first one right where we're standing."

The loan officer dug a cordovan toe into the sand. He frowned as the loose grains gave way like gritty water.

"You can't build on sand," he protested. "It won't take the weight of a high-rise."

"You gotta adjust your thinking if you're gonna do business with me, my friend," Swindell said unctuously. "We're not talking high-rise here. We're talking *low*-rise."

"Huh?"

"Get down on God's beige earth with me, son, and I'll reveal to you the future of real-estate development."

Connors Swindell sank his knees into the sand.

"See this here thermos jug?" he asked.

The banker followed suit, first giving his trouser legs a hitch so the knees wouldn't bag. "Yes."

"Imagine it's a high-rise tower, like the Capitol Records Building back in L.A. But with a penthouse on top. Under a glass shield kinda shaped like a dome. That's this here cap. Are you with me so far, boy? Are you imagining along?"

"I believe I can visualize what you're suggesting," the loan officer said without enthusiasm.

"Now, you watch."

Pawing away a shallow depression in the sand, Connors Swindell thrust the thermos into it. He pushed it down with both hands, rotating it back and forth. The sand hissed in gritty protest. Slowly the thermos sank into the sand until only the clear plastic cup-lid showed.

With careful fingers Connors Swindell smoothed

the sand around the upside-down lip of the cup until only the clear plastic showed.

Swindell flashed him an Ipana grin. "Got the picture now?"

The young loan officer blinked. "I really can't quite grasp what you're trying to convey, Mr. Swindell."

"Almost forgot," said Swindell. He reached into a coat pocket and yanked out two HO-scale human figures. He lifted the cup-lid and placed them inside. Then he reclosed the lid.

The loan officer stared at this for a long time.

"You gettin' it now?" Swindell prompted.

"Condome?" His voice was a parched croak.

"The dome is the penthouse part," Swindell said excitedly. "The guy who lives in the dome pays a premium for all the good healthy sunshine he's gonna have the benefit of. The other ones live down below, where it's nice and cool."

"And dark."

"They got new kinda lights now that simulate daylight. I hear they're good for the old biorhythms. People who work nights use 'em to stay happy." Swindell climbed to his feet to toe sand over a scuttling scorpion, burying it. "For windows, we'll give 'em sand paintings."

The loan officer found his feet, saying, "There is no water in the desert, or electricity."

"We truck in generators. Self-sufficient. And yuppies don't drink common everyday tap water. Everybody knows that."

"But it's out in the middle of nowhere."

"So was Palm Springs. And Las Vegas. They started as dusty villages. But they grew. You know what one of my low-rise Condome towers would be worth planted back in Palm Springs? On dirt-cheap sand?"

The loan officer understood then. But he had one final reservation.

"Mr. Swindell, I think your scheme—I mean, idea—has a certain merit, but you're already in arrears to our bank for over seven million dollars. And that does not include principal."

"Which I ain't never gonna get current on if the condo end of my business goes belly-up," Swindell pointed out firmly.

"I know that. But to lend a man so deeply in debt even more money—"

"So he can climb out of debt and pay you back," Swindell prompted.

"I don't know. The board of directors will be hesitant to extend you additional assistance."

"Then you remind them of a little proverb I heard recently."

"And that is?"

"When a man owes a bank a little money, he's in hot water. But if a man owes the same bank a pile of money—"

"You don't have to finish it, sir."

Swindell did anyway. "The *bank's* in hot water. Wouldn't you rather be in sand?"

"I'll take it up with the board of directors in the morning," the young loan officer said glumly.

Swindell started back to the jeep. "You do that. But I already know what the answer's gonna be. I'm too fucking big to go down."

And he was. Swindell Properties got an immediate line of credit, and construction began that week. The prefab tower went down in one section. It didn't go down as easily as the thermos, but then, it was over two hundred feet long.

It looked to be a sure thing. Then they started losing construction workers to sunstroke and the scorpions. Insurance premiums went through the roof. The Indians sued him not only over the substandard condos but also to recover the now-valuable Condome land, protesting that its true worth had been concealed.

Then the worst blow came.

An engineer brought the bad news to Connors Swindell as he was trying to sink a putt into a tipped wineglass.

"We have a problem, sir," the engineer said gravely.

"Throw a lawyer at it," Swindell had growled. "I'm busy."

"A lawyer won't solve this problem, Mr. Swindell."

Swindell swung. The glass shattered. "What is it?"

"You better come with me."

Swindell followed the man out of his penthouse office, cozily nestled in a great Plexiglas dome in the desert. Instead of leading him through the climate-controlled airlock and out into the desert heat, the chief engineer escorted him to the main Condome elevator.

As they rode the lift down, Swindell noticed for the first time that the engineer's boots were damp. He was about to ask how they got that way when the engineer suddenly hit the kill switch.

The elevator lurched to a stop, nearly upsetting both men.

"What's wrong?" Swindell demanded. "Generator go again?"

"This is as far as we can go."

"What do you mean? This ain't but the twenty-second floor. There's six more to go." He reached for the switch.

"I wouldn't if I were you," the engineer warned.

Swindell hesitated. That was when he heard the water. He looked down. His cowboy boots were swimming in brackish water. It was pouring in through the floor seams.

"Where's this water comin' from!" Swindell howled.

"We think it's an underground stream. Maybe the water table creeping up."

"Water!" Swindell burst out. "In the fucking desert?"

"It happens. Runoff from the mountains has to go somewhere. What doesn't evaporate seeps down into the sand. Sand's porous, you know. Looks like it accumulated down there. Now it's seeping into the Condome shell."

"Take us up! Take us up!" Swindell said, his eyes sick.

As the elevator toiled back to the surface, Connors Swindell felt as if he had left his stomach back in the bowels of the greatest advance in housing since the condominium.

Not to mention his entire future.

They tried everything. Pumping. Sealing up and abandoning the lower six floors. But still the water seeped in.

Swindell ordered a construction slowdown while he scrambled to find a way out of the literal sandtrap he had dug himself into.

"It can't get any worse," Swindell told his secretary after his return from La Plomo, Missouri.

"What is it, Con honey?" asked Constance Payne, whose willingness to get down on the rug and screw her boss remained her chief qualification for the job, even after ten years with Swindell Properties. She wore her hair too red and her sweater too tight.

Swindell looked out from his Palm Springs condo

window. A field of stars spilled across the desert night sky.

"You should have seen that town, baby. As sweet a collection of garrisons and colonials as you ever saw in one spot. Just basking in the sun. Untenanted, fully applianced, with all the sewer, water, and electrical lines a growin' community could ask for. And no one wantin' any part of it because of a little spilt nerve gas."

"Nobody would sell?"

"Naw, I got a few nibbles. But it's soon soon for the grievin' families. I figure I can wait 'em out until they realize they gotta sell to me. But that ain't what I'm talking about. The fool Army came along and tried to decontaminate the whole shebang."

"Is that bad?"

"It is when the decontaminant makes carbolic acid look like Kool-Aid. They started hosing a place down—a sweet little fixer-upper—and the paint just bubbled up and started smoking. Next thing you know, it up and caught fire. Then it exploded. Three million dollars' worth of housing went up in a flash. I lit out right then, it turned my stomach so bad."

Constance Payne pulled her boss down onto her generous lap. "Oh, poor baby," she cooed, playing with his hair.

"Not only that, but I lost Horace."

Her red mouth made a surprised circle. "What happened to Horace?"

"Ingrate up and quit on me."

"That Horace! But you can get another chauffeur."

"Not like Horace. I could trust him. I tell you, baby if things don't turn around soon, the nineties are gonna be a misery."

"Oh, I was hoping you'd be in a good mood when you got back."

"Well, I'm not. So there."

" 'Cause we got another problem."

Swindell brightened. "More paternity suits?" he asked eagerly.

"No, those have kinda settled down."

Swindell's bright smile darkened. "What the hell you been doing all the livelong day, your nails? If we ever gonna get back on our feet, Connie, you gotta do your part."

"I have been. Will you settle down and listen? The Condome is being overrun, or something. The site crew just called it in."

"By who? The bankers?"

"They call themselves Dirt First!!"

"Them mangy curs!" Swindell exploded. "I saw a pack of them back in Missouri. You could smell 'em coming for miles around. What do they want with my Condome?"

"They say you're desecrating the natural habitat of the desert scorpion."

Swindell jumped up so fast his pockets disgorged business cards Velcroed to condom packets.

"Scorpions!" he shouted. "Don't they know scorpions are venomous varmints?"

"I don't think they do. They're painting graffiti on the dome and everything. Should I call your pilot?"

Swindell nodded angrily. "Damn. This is fixin' to be a terrible decade for real estate. I can feel it in my bones."

13

Woody Robbins was in charge of security at Lawrence Livermore Laboratory, an experimental research facility connected with the University of California, and located east of San Francisco.

Even after the cold war had been declared officially over, America's nuclear deterrent force required constant maintenance. East-West tensions may have been reduced to a lulling hum, but the world remained full of nuclear weapons, and where nuclear technology was concerned, Woody Robbins never let down his guard.

Unfortunately, he had just the night shift. The day shift security staff seemed to think that the rare isotopes and spent uranium fuel pellets were kept in secure lead storage containers for controlled access, not for theft protection.

Nuclear material—everything from hair-fine wiring to klystron triggers—was oozing from the brick pores of Lawrence Livermore like sweat from a rotisserie pig.

Tonight Woody Robbins sat at his desk flipping through duty reports and occasionally glancing at a wall-mounted bank of closed-circuit screens that were wired to strategically placed security cameras. But mostly to the portable set on his desk tuned to a Lakers game. Woody was a stickler for security, but the Lakers were important too. Besides, it was a slow night.

Had Woody Robbins happened to tune into the local news instead of a basketball game, he would not have made the mistake of admitting Sky Bluel—who was known to him as a trustworthy UCLA physics major—to the facility. Woody liked Sky, even if she did dress as if the calendar had froze at the Summer of Love.

The ten-o'clock news was showing a clip of Sky Bluel togged out in antique hippie clothes, showing off a tactical neutron bomb whose parts had, with the exception of the breadboard mount—which was an Ace Hardware Washington's Birthday special—come out of Lawrence Livermore, a piece here and a piece there.

But Woody was oblivious of that. The Lakers were down 13 to the Knicks' 61, and it coming on half-time. Woody was worried.

His worries shifted into high gear and an entirely different venue when a microwave-relay van slid up to the gate and the driver accosted the hapless gate guard.

A beeping light under monitor number one brought this unwelcome intrusion to Woody Robbins' attention. He peered past his propped-up feet to the monitor. One look, and all thought of the Lakers fled his mind.

The gate guard was saying something about cameras not being allowed on the grounds except by prior application.

A cameraman responded by shoving a videocam into his face. Its harsh light forced him to turn away.

And a voice that Woody recognized but could

not immediately place demanded to see the head of security.

"Tell him *Twenty-four Hours* is here to inspect his security," intoned the half-familiar baritone voice.

"Oh, Christ," Woody Robbins moaned. "Don Cooder."

He hurried out of his cubicle office without checking the latest score.

Moments later Woody Robbins stood face-to-face with Don Cooder. They stood outside the gate.

"Take your ambush journalism and shove it," Woody said huffily. "I don't answer to you or your network."

"Is that a refusal?" Cooder asked in a threatening tone.

"No," Woody said, showing his teeth in an icily polite smile, "it's an official request for you to go through proper channels."

"Are you aware, Mr. . . . What is your name?"

"Woody," he admitted. "Woody—"

"Are you aware, Mr. Woody, that nuclear materials have been leaking from this facility for months now?"

"I've heard it alleged."

"And what is the source of your knowledge of these events?"

"The guy who's been clobbering you in the ratings, Peter Jennings," Woody returned coolly.

"We'll edit that out later," Cooder mumbled to his cameraman. "Now, about these deadly thefts," he pressed.

"That's an allegation my staff is looking into," Woody said. "I won't advertise an ongoing investigation and risk drying up valuable sources of information."

"You mean cover up for the criminal culprits," snapped Cooder, whose on-air style of speaking was akin to a talking books tabloid.

"There is no cover-up," Woody said testily.

Don Cooder turned to the camera, lifting the microphone to his rugged face.

"When confronted with the startling allegation of Lawrence Livermore materials being used to build a neutron bomb," he intoned seriously, "plant security official Woody hotly denied these charges and proclaimed his innocence."

"Wait a minute! I did not proclaim my innocence!"

Cooder whirled on cue. The mike leapt for Woody Robbins' open mouth like a striking cobra.

"Is that an admission of guilt?" Cooder said eagerly.

"It damn well is not!"

"If you're innocent, you'll let us inspect the premises on behalf of the American taxpapers, now fearful of being nuked by their own tax dollars at work."

"Shove that tax-scare crap," Woody lashed out. "I know your game, Mr. Dead-Last-in-the-Ratings."

Woody waited for the retort that never came. But Don Cooder was for once speechless. His mouth hung as slack as a carp on a hook.

Sky Bluel selected that moment to approach the gate.

Woody was so surprised to see her that he too was struck speechless. But only for a moment.

"Good evening, Miss Bluel," he said in a forced-polite voice.

"I need to do some after-hours work," Sky Bluel said tightly, eyeing Don Cooder uncertainly. "Is it okay?"

Woody smiled. "Always."

Sky Bluel was passed with a longer-than-usual

glance at her plant security card, but she was passed.

"Where were we?" Don Cooder asked, suddenly mollified.

Woody noted the appreciative gleam in his eye. The jerk, he thought, he's old enough to be her damn father.

Sky Bluel was passed at the main desk, as well. She hurried to the lab where she did her work with neutron-bombardment applications. But she lingered there only a moment.

Beyond the lab was a nuclear storage area. Donning a radiation-proof coverall suit, she entered through the double doors, which responded to her magnetic passcard.

It was the work of a few minutes to acquire a spherical beryllium-oxide tamper and a corresponding amount of tritium isotope and gingerly place them into a lead-lined carrying container.

Sky grinned. Jane Fonda would be so proud, if she only knew. Maybe they would end up on *Letterman* together.

Woody Robbins thought he was finally getting through to Don Cooder.

"You say you really have no idea," Cooder was saying. "Let me be sure I have this straight, now. Really no idea what, if anything, in the way of nuclear materials, has been stolen—I mean allegedly stolen—from Lawrence Livermore?"

"That's right," Woody said, relaxing slightly, becoming aware of the *tap-tap* of a woman's booted feet coming up behind him. "It's a very involved inventory process complicated by the fact that nuclear materials as they are processed are used up. They diminish. Separating use loss from shrinkage is involved. Excuse me," he added, turning toward the footsteps.

Don Cooder's darkly handsome black Irish face fell into a glower.

"Shrinkage!" he exploded, drowning out all other sounds. "Dangerous fusion material!"

"Fission, not fusion," Woody corrected tightly. "We don't do fusion at Lawrence Livermore."

"—dangerous fissionable materials are possibly in the hands of rabid terrorists and you have the gall to call it shrinkage?" Cooder finished hotly. "Nukes are not mere white goods and this isn't a department store, Mr. Woody!"

"Listen, you have no right making these irresponsible allegations!" Woody retorted. "Now, for the last time, either get out, get clearance to enter lawfully, or I'll have to take steps. We can't leave this gate open like this."

"Afraid something will slip through under your very nose?" asked Don Cooder as the videocam whirred on, and a dark figure lugged a heavy satchel way down the road.

"No!" Woody said, storming off, fists bunched in white-knuckled anger.

The video camera lingered on him as he secured the gate.

Woody endured the annoying video light until it finally winked out. The news crew boarded the van. Then the van backed away with all the agile grace of a retreating rhinoceros.

As Woody stormed back to his cubicle office, needing a change of shirt, a memory tickled the back of his mind.

What was it now? he wondered. Something he was about to do.

The Lakers game was still under way when he

got back. The score was now 89 to 26, Lakers trailing. He settled in behind his battle-scarred desk.

The memory came back. Who was the woman who had slipped by the gate when he was arguing with that damned Cooder?

Then he remembered Sky Bluel. "Had to be her," he muttered, relaxing. "Nice kid." The future was brighter with gals like her coming out of UCLA. Too bad she was stuck in the past like that.

Sky Bluel walked and walked as she had been instructed, the heavy lead carrying container dragging her right arm practically out of its socket. She glanced over her shoulder several times, feeling exhilarated. It was just like the sixties, which she thought she could dimly remember, having been born in November 1969.

All her life, Sky Bluel had listened to her parents' tales of the sixties. It made her feel inadequate, as if she were born a generation too late. Her consciousness level was high, but wasted. There was so little to protest against. And almost no one to do it with.

But when her graduate work brought her to Lawrence Livermore, Sky was horrified to discover how lax the facility was. At last she had found a cause. Disarmament. It was an old cause, true, but with a fresh new twist.

People had grown apathetic. Her own generation was hopelessly yuppified. But Sky would show them that disarmament was more important than ever. Especially with all the crazy terrorists troubling the world.

And so she had built her own neutron bomb. She had selected the La Plomo incident as the grand backdrop against which she would expose the horrible truth that would galvanize her generation into the new antinuclear movement: unnuking.

Yes, it had gone awry, but Don Cooder had showed her a better way to attack the problem.

And she had done it. She now carried the necessary tritium isotope. She knew she would succeed. Had she not worn her mother's very own love beads, actually bought at Woodstock? And were these not the very same blue jeans her father had worn when he tried to levitate the Pentagon in 1973 to protest the unjust Vietnam war?

Who could fail with such a heritage?

The approaching headlights brought her worried face back again.

She released a gleeful squeal of delight. It was the network van. Sky recognized the network fish-eye symbol.

"Hop in," said Don Cooder, rolling back the side sliding door.

He took the container. Sky climbed in. And the van roared off.

"We did it! We did it!" she said excitedly. "This is so far out its absolutely the most."

"This is just the groovy beginning," said Don Cooder proudly. He preened himself in a mirror in preparation for doing a quick two-shot on the successful liberation of unsecured nuclear material.

The comb got stuck in his oversprayed hair. It refused to budge. He pulled harder. He grunted like a woman in labor.

"Oh, my God," Sky cried in horror. "Won't it come loose?"

"Not to worry," Cooder said manfully. "Occupational hazard. I know exactly what to do."

And using a pair of wire cutters, he snipped the comb to pieces, leaving only a small square section of caught teeth.

"Are you going to just leave it there?" Sky asked as Cooder patted down the affected area.

"It's in the back of the head," Cooder explained. "No one ever sees the back of an anchor's head. I'll have it professionally removed later. The network has special technicians on staff for just this kind of thing."

He lifted the microphone as the video cameraman maneuvered around to shoot Cooder over Sky's shoulder.

"Ready?" he asked.

Sky Bluel swallowed. She thought she was ready, ready for anything. But this was getting truly weird. She hated weird. Weird wasn't where it was at.

14

The flight from San Francisco to the California resort town of Palm Springs was relatively short. Barely an hour. But to Remo Williams it was as interminable as a death.

First, it was the silence. Technically, they were not on the job, so Chiun felt it acceptable to lapse into one of his moody silences again, and nothing Remo said could bring him out of it.

The cabin temperature seemed chillier than normal to Remo, who had changed into a fresh T-shirt en route to the airport.

"Does this have anything to do with the Mongols?" Remo ventured. "I did kinda show you up during our little treasure hunt in China."

Chiun looked out upon the night lights passing below with opaque regard.

"I'll take that as a no," Remo said. "Whatever I did, I must have done it after that."

Chiun twitched slightly.

Remo made a mental note that he was getting warmer.

"I know I was on my best behavior at the village," he added, "so that can't be it."

The twitch came again, more pronounced.

Hot, Remo thought. I'm definitely hot.

His mind went back to the weeks they had spent in the village of Sinanju. On the whole it had been a much less tumultuous stay than any in the past. They had arrived with hundreds of Mongols bearing the treasure of Genghis Khan. This was divided between the House of Sinanju and the Golden Horde with great ceremony. Remo thought to himself that Chiun had clipped the Mongols out of the best artifacts, but had said nothing. Treasure didn't excite him. The treasure trove had been borne away at the end of the first week. Half the Mongols had stayed to continue the celebration. Most were too drunk from quaffing fermented goat's milk and wine to ride anyway. Day by day they had drifted away until only a core group had remained. Chiun had not begun ignoring him until after they finally departed, Remo recalled.

But he could remember nothing he had said or done since that time that might have offended the Master of Sinanju. Then he recalled Chiun's remark made back in Rye that it was something he had not done. Remo frowned. What had he not done? The infinite possibilities staggered him.

Remo decided to take another tack.

"Tell me a story, Little Father."

"I am not speaking with you presently," Chiun said coldly.

"I'm not looking for conversation," Remo said with forced good nature. "I meant a legend. You know, a good old-fashioned Sinanju legend, like you used to tell me in the old days. You've been telling me fewer and fewer legends these days."

"Legends are for the educable," Chiun snapped.

"Aw, come on. Just one. A short one. Maybe something that covers the mission."

"I do not know of any such legend. In the history

of Sinanju we have never dealt with neutral booms or mud people or bathers in urine."

"Please?" Remo said. "I hate to admit this, but I kinda miss those old legends of yours."

Chiun's set features softened like wax hovering at its melting point.

"You might find the lesson of Master Vimu particularly instructive," he allowed in a quieter tone.

"So, tell it," Remo prompted.

"Look it up," Chiun said, compressing his mouth in a manner that suggested aeons of silence to come.

Remo folded his arms. He hit the seat-recline button and settled back. "Count on it," he growled.

The moment they were on the ground, Chiun began speaking again.

"It is almost eleven o'clock," he said.

"Yeah, it's late. I hope we can get a rental this late."

"I mean it is nearly time for the eleven-o'clock news."

Remo snapped his fingers. "Your press conference!" he said suddenly. "Too bad, Little Father. Out here they don't have eleven-o'clock news. The late news comes on at ten."

"You mean I have wasted my breath on those lunatic press persons for nothing!" he fumed.

"Join the legion of past victims," Remo said, entering the airport lounge.

An airline representative told him that the only rental agent was a convenient quarter-mile down the road.

"Convenience," Remo told her glumly, "means *in* the airport. Not near it."

"I just work for the airline," she told him.

They took a cab to the rental agency. Remo paid

off the cab and pushed into the counter area, almost tripping over the body.

The body lay in the middle of the floor. Remo knelt beside the man, quickly ascertaining that he had died of multiple spike wounds. He knew it was a spike because one stuck up from his head like a rusty pumpkin stem.

"Either Palm Springs has a serious vampire problem or Dirt First has been here," Remo told the Master of Sinanju.

Chiun stared at the body with flinty eyes. "Why has this man been crucified, Remo?"

"Who knows?" Remo said, looking around the empty office. "Maybe in the dark they mistook him for a sequoia."

"This is clear proof of their perfidy."

"They'll pay for it," Remo promised, lifting a key off the counter rack. The round metal tag matched the license plate of a white sedan they commandeered from the parking lot.

Remo sent it out into the desert, his face angry.

"Master Vimu, huh?" Remo said as they rode under a California desert moon. "Care to hum a few bars just to get me started?"

"You could not carry the tune," Chiun told him, falling silent once more.

Connors Swindell loved toys. Big ones. At the height of his career in development, he got to play with real wrecking balls, bulldozers, and concrete-eating pneumatic nibblers.

The last toy he was going to relinquish, he vowed to himself, was his personal helicopter.

Once he had had a small fleet of them stationed at strategic nerve centers, the better to visit the many construction sites he had had, in his glory days, sprinkled all over the country.

Now Swindell was down to one active site, a handful of overpriced condos, and one helicopter. And he would be damned if he would lose this handy little eggbeater to his creditors.

It was a scarlet-and-cream Sikorsky, and it ferried him from his private Palm Springs roof pad into the desert.

"We ought to be coming up on it any minute now," the pilot was saying.

"About damn time," Swindell told him.

"She may need an overhaul," the pilot added.

"What makes you say that?"

"The balance is off. She's flying a little rotor-heavy."

"Seems all right to me. A nice smooth little ride, as always."

"Oh, there's no danger. It's just that you get sensitive to the feel of these birds, and this one's gone tail-heavy."

"Let me worry about maintenance," Swindell snapped. "You just earn your flight pay."

"Yes, sir," the pilot said unhappily.

Twenty minutes later, the pilot's voice came in the earphones with more than a suggestion of edginess.

"Umm, Mr. Swindell . . ." he began.

"What?"

"We've overshot the site. I don't know how it happened, but we should have overflown it ten minutes ago."

"You on course?" Swindell asked, more perplexed than angry.

"Absolutely. By the compass."

Swindell looked out the bubble. "I didn't see any floodlights," he said uneasily. The rotor chopping made his teeth vibrate.

"Same here. Do you suppose they're out?"

"Out?" Swindell asked. "We have our own generators. And backups. How could both go out?" He looked down through the chin port.

Swindell's mouth dropped like a steam shovel's jaw. It hung there, agape. Then he answered his own question. "Those damn Dirt Firsters!" he snarled.

There was only one road snaking through the Little San Bernardino Mountains into the desert. So Remo knew he stood little chance of becoming lost. He knew that the Condome site, like most construction sites, would be ablaze with floodlights to minimize pilferage of the open-air material stockpiles.

Remo saw no floodlights.

But he did smell something unpleasantly familiar—the combined body odor of a dozen unwashed human beings.

"We're close. Real close," Remo told Chiun.

"I see nothing," Chiun said petulantly.

"Take a whiff. The Dirt Firsters are in this area. If they're close, so is the Condome project."

"I do not know this word 'Condome.' "

"Welcome to America in the nineties," Remo sighed. "I'm still trying to transcend Madonna."

"Your religion is your concern," Chiun sniffed.

If there was any doubt Dirt First!! was in the vicinity, the sight of Day-Glo yellow blotches on passing palm boles dispelled that. They marked fresh spikes. The occasional broken-armed cactus stood as mute testimony to Dirt First's attempt to adapt their environmental consciences to the desert.

"We'd better hurry before the cholla cactus ends up on the endangered-succulent list," Remo muttered.

Remo discovered the presence of a Dirt Firster

blocking the road in an unmistakable way: he almost ran one down.

His headlights picked up a woman's wounded-deer eyes in a near-invisible face. Remo had mistaken her for a road kill because she lay across the road like a human log coated with sand.

"Hang on!" Remo called, wrenching the wheel to the left. The car sailed off the road and into a dune. It bounced along before coming to a stop, oil pan scraping sand.

Remo killed the ignition and plunged out of the car. He wasn't sure if he had struck the woman or not.

When she sat up and shook a sandy fist in his direction, he received his answer.

"You idiot!" she complained. "You almost ran me over!"

"You're lying across a dark road practically in camouflage and you're calling *me* an idiot?" Remo snapped back. "You're damn lucky a tire didn't burst that melon you think is your head."

"I happen to be monkey-wrenching," she said tartly, examining her beaded Indian skirt for damage.

"Committing suicide is a better term for it," Remo said, roughly pulling the woman to her feet.

"We call it monkey-wrenching. Impeding undesirable progress in the cause of Mother Nature."

"And I call this getting to the heart of the matter," Remo said, suddenly twisting the woman's plump wrist in a painful direction.

"Ow! Ow! This isn't fair."

"Losing a nuke always brings out the worst in me," Remo snapped. "Right, Chiun?"

The Master of Sinanju floated up to examine the woman's squirming figure. She noticed him and in the dark made a misidentification.

"Hey, Desert Chief. How about telling your pale-face friend to let a blood sister go? I ain't done nothing."

Chiun looked his question.

"She thinks you're an Indian," Remo supplied.

Chiun grimaced. "The woman is blind," he said. "But I will open her eyes." One yellow claw of a hand drifted out to her earlobe, took a pinch, and slowly increased the pressure.

The Dirt Firster's reaction was not that of a person with a pinched earlobe, but one who had somehow gotten her tongue caught in a light socket. Flinging out her arms, she howled as if to raise the dead.

"First question," Remo said. "Where are the rest of them?"

"Over . . . there," she gasped. "At the . . . ow . . . Condome. Monkey-wrenching it. Please! That's my triple-pierced ear!"

"Second question. Pay attention. This is important. Who has the neutron bomb?"

"Umm, Russia?"

"Wrong."

"China? The U.S.? I'm not big on current events."

"You can do better than that," Remo warned.

"How should I know?" she asked, squeezing her eyes.

"You're with Dirt First," Remo explained. "We know they lifted the bomb. Is it here?"

"Nobody told me about any bomb. Honest Injun."

Remo frowned. He turned to the Master of Sinanju. "She sounds like she's telling the truth," he said reluctantly.

"I am telling the truth, you conterprogressive!"

"Third and last question," Remo said. "Did your people gas La Plomo?"

"No!" Tears streamed down her face, making flesh-colored vein patterns on her dirty cheeks.

Remo watched as Chiun applied increasing pressure. When the woman simply repeated "No!" several times in quick succession, Chiun shifted his tormenting hand to the base of her spine. He gave a tap. The woman flopped to the road like a bouncy sack of suet. She did not get up again.

"What did you do that for?" Remo demanded. "We didn't get any answers."

"Yes, we did," Chiun said tightly. "We learned the truth."

"Yeah? Well, maybe she wasn't in on it. They recruit new people all the time." Remo looked away. "Okay, let's shake up the rest of them."

They went in search of the Condome site.

Fabrique Foirade was immensely proud of himself.

After another ignominious retreat, he had regrouped his forces and shifted tactics with what he believed was the oppression-honed brilliance of a Ho Chi Minh.

"Okay," he had said. "Now they know we're serious. They're cowering in that ugly dome of a thing. So we fall back on some good old-fashioned monkey-wrenching."

"Like what?" he was asked.

"First, we fill the gas tanks of every vehicle with sand."

"But we didn't bring any sand!"

"We're standing on tons," Fabrique pointed out.

Everyone noticed this for a fact.

"Gee, if we use real desert sand, won't that wreck the local ecosystem?" Fabrique was asked.

This point was hotly debated for several moments. Fabrique Foirade won the argument by the simple expedient of braining the most vocal dissenter with the blunt end of a handy spike.

"Any other objections?" he inquired stonily.

He received none. Fabrique took this as a textbook example of the perfect application of socialist dialogue.

"Okay," he urged, "sand in the tanks. Cut every wire and break every tool. And somebody dump Joyce across the road as an obstruction. She'll know what to do when she wakes up."

This proved to be easy enough to accomplish. The surplus of sand was a tremendous boon. Soon the outside gas generators were sputtering into silence. The lights died out.

"Maybe we should have saved the light for last," a man who was so coated with sand that he resembled walking sandpaper suggested timidly, after the overwhelming darkness put a stop to further ecotage. Dirt First!! kept bumping into one another.

Someone found a battery-powered flashlight. Foirade took possession of this and started rooting around. The others merrily broke everything the light illuminated.

"Hold it!" Fabrique cried, fishing the light around a wooden shack. "I found a bunch of paint."

The others joined in. Behind them the construction workers were pounding on the electronic airlock door. Without power, it refused to open. They were trapped.

And so they watched, helpless and profane, as the minions of Dirt First!! formed a fire-bucket brigade and ferried dozens of paint cans to the clear dome itself.

Brushes were brought up. Paint-can lids opened. The Dirt Firsters gathered around the dome and began painting three-foot-high slogans in praise of natural beauty—all of which were lost on the trapped construction workers, inasmuch as, from their vantage points, the letters were backward.

Some of them, witnessing the desecration of months of painstaking work undertaken in the worst construction climate of their lives, wept bitterly as the flawless Plexiglas collected oversize streaks of clumsily applied paint.

Others turned away. Still others pounded at the inner Plexiglas walls, as if they could shatter the impenetrable stuff and knock out the grinning teeth of the desert raiders only inches away, in clear view but beyond retribution.

Then something strange happened.

A grinning Dirt Firster shoved his face against the Plexiglas. They had been doing that all along to taunt the construction crew. But this one actually struck the transparent material with enough force to make it reverberate like a bell.

When the face withdrew, it left a smear of red that was not paint. He had been using green paint. Slipping down the rilling red liquid were two white Chicklet-like teeth.

The Dirt Firster hit the ground, his legs bouncing high before they struck the sand for the final time.

"What happened to him?" Ed Coyne muttered in surprise.

Before anyone could venture a guess, another Dirt First!! protester suddenly leapt very high into the air. He landed in the exact center of the Condome dome. Facedown. He didn't move after he struck. He just lay splayed there like a weary scarecrow. His nose formed a silver-dollar-size pancake in his face. It hadn't been that shape a moment before.

A cheer went up among the construction workers.

For out in the night, two fleet shapes went among the Dirt Firsters, wreaking havoc.

One was a lean man in a white T-shirt. Moonlight showed that much, no more.

The other was a wispily tiny figure in phantom gray.

The construction crew raced back and forth inside the dome, trying to follow the action. The pair seemed always to be one step ahead.

"Over here!" a man would shout. But by the time the crew surged to the spot, all that remained was a twitching body.

Once they caught a glimpse of a thick-wristed hand reaching out from the darkness to take a Dirt Firster by the back of the neck and use his long hair to clean off a particularly obscene scrawl. The Dirt Firster's face moved faster than it seemed possible for a face to move. And the crew realized it was simply because the motivating hand was moving with lightning speed.

In a twinkling, the wet scrawl was gone. So was the guy in the white T-shirt.

The Dirt Firster's face, now wet and Day-Glo orange, collapsed to the sand like a cast-off rag.

"Who are these guys?" Ed Coyne asked in awe.

"Who cares! Let's see what they do next."

What they did next was to make short work of the remaining members of Dirt First!!

Bodies flew in all directions. One man attempted to use a spike to defend himself from the wispy one in gray.

The attacker came on, spike held high. A single finger, somehow too long to be human, snaked up to intercept the descending instrument. The spike spat a spark and lost its point.

The Dirt Firster next tried to nail the one in gray with the ragged stump.

The ragged stump somehow changed direction in

mid-stroke, taking a grasping hand along with it. It knocked out a savagely grinning row of teeth.

The man stumbled off, trying not to swallow the spike whole.

Then the excitement subsided. The victorious pair faded back from the dome as if unwilling to take a bow, despite the cheers and whistles and thunderous applause that shook the dome.

At that point a searchlight raked the dome. The crew looked up to see a familiar scarlet Sikorsky helicopter descend from the clear desert sky.

They sobered instantly, wondering if they would still be employed in the morning. A few thought the spectacle they had witnessed was worth the loss of pay.

15

Remo Williams thought he had gotten most of them.

As another Dirt Firster bit the sand, a loose bag of broken bones, he looked around for Chiun. There was no sign of the Master of Sinanju on this side of the dome.

Then he caught a fleeting glimpse of gray silk through the transparent edge of the dome.

Circling, Remo came upon Chiun about to dispatch a scrawny Dirt Firster like a farmer harvesting a chicken.

Holding the man by the neck, but using only the awesome pressure of his impossibly long nails, the Master of Sinanju prepared to give a wrenching twist.

"Hold up, Chiun."

Chiun turned, pulling his intended victim along. "Why?" he demanded. "I am about to mete out justice to this foul murderer of rental agents."

"Not to mention farmers," Remo said grimly.

"He is not responsible for that," Chiun said flatly.

"We'll see. First, he tells us where the bomb is."

"Bomb?" asked Fabrique Foirade, his heart pounding high in his throat. He squirmed in the old

Oriental's grip, but it was like his neck was impaled by a circle of supersharp darning needles. One wrong move might rip his own windpipe or sever his jugular.

"The neutron bomb," said the skinny guy. "Where is it?" Fabrique recognized him from La Plomo. The reactionary. It was amazing how well he could discern people now that he no longer wore his hair over his face like an unkempt Pekingese.

"Search me," he muttered, trembling.

"We know you and your walking mud pies stole the neutron bomb," Remo retorted. "Your filthy handprints were all over the pickup truck it was last seen on."

"Get real, man." Fabrique sneered. "It was abandoned. We just tried to salvage it, you know, for the ride home. I don't know about any neutron bomb—except they aren't kind to flowers and other living things."

"I suppose you don't know about the dead guy we found by the pickup, either?" Remo asked.

"Just that he was a really, really cool dude. Cool to the touch, that is. He was already dead when we got there."

Remo took a chance. "Can the crap. We have proof he was a Dirt Firster."

"Fat chance. He was so clean it was obscene. Mud is our blood! Our blood is mud!" he chanted.

Remo and Chiun exchanged bemused looks.

"My method is better," Chiun suggested.

"Little Father," Remo said, stepping back, "be my guest."

"It will be a pleasure to wring the truth from such a one as this specimen," said the Master of Sinanju gravely. "But he does not know the answers we seek."

Then, like a spiked dog collar turned inside out,

the terrible needles began to close on Fabrique Foirade's scrawny neck.

The Dirt Firster had only begun to empty his lungs in a fearful scream when the scarlet helicopter descended, kicking up dust in whirling, stinging billows.

"Now what?" Remo said, throwing his forearm over his mouth and nose. He squeezed his eyes shut. The light from the helicopter turned the inside of his eyelids reddish-pink.

"Remo," Chiun called over the noise, "catch the dirty one! He is coming toward you!"

"Catch him? I thought *you* had him."

"I did—until this manmade dust storm was called down upon my poor head," Chiun pointed out in a squeaky voice.

"Wonderful," Remo muttered. Eyes closed, he lashed out, trying to gather up the air around him. But between the sound and the sand, he succeeded only in getting his forearms thoroughly sandblasted.

The rotor whine died. When the sand stopped peppering his squinched-up face, Remo finally opened his eyes. They glared with dark anger. He looked around.

The helicopter had settled. The Master of Sinanju was lowering his full kimono sleeves. Unconcernedly he brushed the loose sand that had collected in the folds of his robe.

There was no sign of the escaped Dirt Firster.

"Great, you lost him," Remo said, looking around in vain.

"Blame that one," Chiun said, pointing to the thick-bodied man stepping from the scarlet helicopter.

"Thank you, I will," Remo said, starting for the

helicopter. He recognized the man's toothy grin and pinkie-ring diamond.

"What's going on here?" Connors Swindell demanded hotly.

"I just broke up the west-coast chapter of Dirt First!!" Remo told him flatly.

"Nice breaking," Swindell said appreciatively, stepping over a moaning body. Then, catching a good glimpse of Remo's lean face in the helicopter floodlight, he squinted. "Don't I know you?"

"You handed me a condom back at La Plomo."

Swindell brightened. "You use it yet?"

"No."

"Have another. Nothing short of an airbag beats 'em for accident prevention, and between you and me, I ain't airbag size myself."

Folding his arms angrily, Remo ignored the offered packet. The Master of Sinanju drifted up behind Swindell. His dark kimono was all but invisible in the backglow, giving him the appearance of a disembodied head floating in the night.

"Mind explaining what you're doing out here?" Remo asked tightly.

"Doin'?" Swindell said huffily. "I come to protect my baby from harm." Swindell's beefy bediamonded hand swept out to encompass the moon-burnished Condome and its trapped construction crew, huddling like shadowy specimens in some futuristic zoo.

"This!" Remo asked in surprise. "This is *yours?*"

"You ain't heard that?" Swindell returned, equally shocked. "Where you been lately—Outer Mongolia?"

"As a matter of fact, yeah," Remo returned.

His words were drowned out by the rising whine of the helicopter turbine.

"What the hell?" Swindell barked, turning. "Shut that down! You shut that down, hear?"

Instead of replying, the white-faced helicopter pilot sent the Sikorsky lifting clear of the sand. Through narrowed eyes Remo could see why. The escaped Dirt Firster crouched behind him, pressing a railroad spike into his gulping Adam's apple.

"Don't look now," Remo said glumly, "but Dirt First just hijacked your helicopter."

"What!" Swindell's voice was a scream. It tore through Remo's ear. "Not my baby. He can't! I ain't got another!"

He turned to Remo, frantic, grabbing his shirt front. "You gotta stop it!" he pleaded. "You just gotta!"

"How?" Remo asked, gazing skyward at the rising chopper. "Lasso it with a handy jungle vine?"

The pilot was evidently too nervous to manage the delicate controls correctly. Hanging low in the night, the chopper wobbled, as if about to fall.

"I'll pay!" Swindell shrieked. "Anything! To anyone! It's my last chopper!"

The Master of Sinanju piped up loudly, "What is your offer?"

Swindell swing on Chiun, face twisting. In an imploring voice he shouted, "You got a free condo! How's that grab you?"

"Sold!" said the Master of Sinanju, bending down to pick up a flat sheet of scrap metal. Straightening, he hefted it, as if testing its weight. Then, one arm snapping back, he let fly.

Like a square Frisbee, the metal scrap scaled up for the rear rotor. It bounced off the spinning disk with a snarling clang, dropping back mangled. Shards of rotor came down with it.

Without the stabilizing effect of the tail rotor pushing against the main rotor's torque, the helicopter began spinning counterclockwise, like a top on a string.

"Get back!" Remo shouted. "It's going to crash!"

Everyone on the ground jumped clear.

The helicopter pilot instantly realized what the problem was. Reaching up, he cut the main rotor. Disengaged, the auto-rotating blades acted like a parachute, allowing the ship to settle with only a jar.

Unfortunately, it landed on a dune at an angle. Rotors still turning, it teetered, then fell over. The rotor dashed itself out of shape against the sand, throwing up stinging grit.

A section of rotor broke off and shattered the Plexiglas bubble, which instantly turned red, inside and out.

Then there was only silence.

Remo was the first to reach the stricken helicopter. He plunged in through the open door.

The cockpit was a mess of tangled instrumentation and human remains. The Dirt Firster had gotten the worst of it. The rotor shard had bisected his torso from neck to hip at an oblique angle. He lay in two main pieces. A few fingers were scattered here and there, and one whole hand, clutching a spike, lay wedged under one of the directional control pedals.

"Looks like he tried to fend it off," Remo muttered, noting that the violence of the rotor strike had blown dirt and sand dust off the Dirt Firster. Even his blood was dirty.

Chiun, standing outside, nodded in satisfaction. "He is as dead as Mic Vorrow."

"Who?"

"The famous dead helicopter actor," said Chiun.

"Oh, that Mic Vorrow," Remo said, checking the pilot.

"How bad is it?" Connors Swindell called from a distance.

"You're gonna need another helicopter pilot," Remo called back, noting the pilot's glassy stare.

"Damn! That's two employees I lost just today. This is sure gonna be one miserable decade."

Remo stepped from the wreckage. "How's that?" he asked, trotting back to Connors Swindell.

"Lost my chauffeur. Been with me years." Swindell gave the mangled aircraft a frightened squint. "Won't the helicopter blow up?"

"I doubt it," Remo said, looking back. Chiun remained with the helicopter, examining it intently. After a brief glance at the dead, he concentrated on the shattered exterior, sniffing like a curious kitten.

"What's your friend doing?" Swindell asked curiously.

"Probably screwing things up worse than they already are," Remo grumbled. "Look, I have some questions for you." Remo handed him a card that said he was Remo Goolsby of the CIA.

"CIA agents carry cards?" Swindell asked, returning the card.

"This one does," Remo told him. "I'm investigating the La Plomo disaster."

"Crying shame," Swindell said piously. "All them fine homeowners. Snuffed out in their sleep like that."

"So what were you doing there?"

"Checking out property. Anytime you gotta disaster like that, lots of property changes hands. I'm in real estate. Did you get one of my cards?" He flashed one of his condom-packet business cards.

"Keep it," Remo said. "We think Dirt First!! was responsible for the poison-gas attack at La Plomo."

"You know," Swindell said slowly, "I was thinking the same thing myself." He smiled broadly. "So if two right smart individuals like you and me come to that independent conclusion, well, now, it must be so, don't it?"

"We also think they hijacked the neutron bomb that girl brought to La Plomo. Since they're here, it stands to reason the neutron bomb is somewhere here too."

Swindell started. "Damn! Should we evacuate?"

"That's a good first step. Can you get me inside that thing?"

Swindell winced. "Thing? That, my friend, is a Condome. And you and your little Chinese friend are the proud owners of one of our top residential units. Since you done me a good turn, and all."

Remo frowned. "But the helicopter was destroyed."

"I give a man credit for trying, I surely do." Swindell laid a heavy arm across Remo's shoulders. He nudged Remo away from the helicopter. "Tell you what, to show there's no hard feelings, I'm gonna give you your choice of ground-floor units."

Remo regarded the Condome blankly. "Does that mean the top or the bottom?"

"Bottom. I keep forgettin' to adjust the terminology." Swindell's eyes shifted back to Chiun's searching figure. "Why don't I let you and your friend do a thorough search of the Condome? And if you don't find that little lost neutron bomb of yours inside, we can do an open house. Maybe you can tell your friends about this fine opportunity to live like folks will in the twenty-first century."

Remo turned to Chiun. "Hey, Little Father. Come on. If the bomb is anywhere, it's probably in the dome."

The Master of Sinanju was sniffing at a hatch in the helicopter's thick boom.

"Chiun, you hear me?" he shouted in exasperation.

"I have found it," Chiun called distantly.

Swindell grabbed Remo's arm. "Come on, let's not waste any more time. That bad old bomb could go off any second now."

"Found what?" Remo said, his arm slipping from Swindell's hands as if intangible.

"The neutral boom," Chiun replied brittlely.

"What!" Remo flashed to the Master of Sinanju's side, leaving Swindell's outstretched arm hanging on empty air. Swindell pounded after him, huffing and puffing as if going into cardiac arrest. The night air was cool but his toothy face broke out in little dewlike droplets of sweat. Even his teeth seemed to sweat.

As Remo drew near, the Master of Sinanju slipped his nails into the slightly ajar crack in the helicopter's tail boom. A hatch popped down.

And out of the black space tumbled the missing neutron bomb. It plopped into the sand with a mushy thump, like a silver trophy on an overdone base.

"Oh, Lordy." Connors Swindell gave a twisted moan. "Get away from it! It might go up!"

"It's okay," Remo assured him, touching the electronics. "Just relax."

Swindell paced back and forth like his shoes hurt. "This is awful! This is terrible! I don't wanna be nuked."

"Will you relax?" Remo told him. "It's not armed. I know how these things work. Not all the plastique charges are in place. It can't go nuclear without them all."

"I say we take no chances," the Master of Sinanju said.

"I second that," Remo said grimly. And stepping

up to the silvery sphere, he began extracting plastique charges by their convenient handles.

Swindell howled in anguish. "What are you doing? Are you crazy? Let experts handle this! We gotta hightail it!"

"Get a grip, will you?" Remo shot back. "There's no danger."

When he had reduced the device to a skeleton of welded rings, Remo started in on the framework. Metal broke with snapping barks. Soon it lay stripped to the beryllium-oxide tamper. That, Remo left alone. He didn't know what would happen if he breached it.

"Well," Remo said, stepping back and slapping his hands clean, "that's the end of that. The mystery's solved. Dirt First!! stole the bomb and now it's neutralized."

Connors Swindell suddenly lost his anguished look. His fleshy face loosened, then relaxed. He stopped his mad pacing.

"That's the best damn news I've heard all decade," he said in joyous relief.

Remo turned to Chiun. "Nice detecting. How'd you guess it was in the helicopter? I would have sworn he didn't have enough time to grab the bomb and take it with him."

"I did not guess," Chiun said, eyeing Connors Swindell narrowly, "I detected the telltale scent of the explosives."

"You must have a great nose."

"I have excellent judgment."

"Ready to admit Dirt First!! was behind this all along?" Remo suggested happily.

"No," said the Master of Sinanju, turning his back on Remo and Connors Swindell. "Show me my well-deserved reward. It may be I will occupy it very soon."

And casting a narrow glance to Remo, he floated toward the Condome.

"We're having a little tiff," Remo explained for Swindell's benefit. "Don't take him too seriously."

"I take every potential buyer seriously," he said, taking out a white silk handkerchief and mopping his brow until it was wet enough to wring. "Especially when he can bring down an entire helicopter with a hunk of tin flashing."

16

When Remo Williams liberated the construction crew from the frozen Condome airlock, they poured out, waving hammers and other heavy tools.

"Monkey wrenching!" cried a man who carried an actual ten-pound monkey wrench like a broadsword. "I'll show them monkey wrenching."

There weren't enough living Dirt Firsters to pound on, so the crew vented their wrath on the scorpion population.

"I need to use your phone," Remo told Connors Swindell, who couldn't figure out which fascinated him more—the ferocity of his crew or the strange way the skinny CIA agent had opened the airlock door. Since the power was out, it had been frozen in place. The skinny guy had used the side on his hand to chop out a section of Plexiglas, exposing the locking mechanism. Then, simply reaching in, he manipulated the lock.

The great door had opened as easily as a refrigerator, and they all made room for the furious outpouring of frustrated men.

"How'd you do that?" Swindell wondered, escortint them through the massive bank-vault-like airlock.

"I used to be lock picker for the CIA," Remo said blandly.

"But you used your hands."

"Had to. Left my picks back in Mongolia. Now how about that phone?"

"If we can find a cellular, you're all set."

They found a cellular phone in the penthouse complex. Swindell proudly led Remo and Chiun into his lavish penthouse office. His face fell as Remo went to the phone without commenting on the tasteful interior decoration and gracious living spaces.

Undaunted, he turned the charm on Chiun instead. "Yessir, I think any man would be right proud to live in digs like these. Don't you?"

"Possibly," Chiun undertoned. His eyes were slits.

Swindell didn't like the way the little Asian was eyeing him. It was creepy. Like he could see right through him. And Connors Swindell prided himself on being as transparent as chilled steel.

"You'll change your tune once you see one of the nice units I got picked out just for you," he said. "Yessir, Con Swindell don't forget a favor. You and you CIA friend saved my Condome from being nuked by those crazy anarchists. And I ain't never gonna forget it."

"Let us repair to another room."

"Why's that?"

"My son has a secret call to make."

"Oh, I get it. CIA stuff. Come on, I'll show you the kitchen. It's got every modern convenience known to man."

"Does it have a spittoon? I have noticed during my years in this land that spittoons are a rare luxury."

"No, but it's got a mean microwave."

"Rice cannot be microwaved."

Swindell blinked. "What's that got to do with the price of real estate?" he wondered, leading the old man away.

Once alone, Remo dialed Harold W. Smith.

"Mission accomplished, Smitty."

"You located the neutron device?" Smith asked eagerly.

"Located and dislocated," Remo said proudly. "It's in pieces. Should I bring them back?"

"Yes, do that. I do not want nuclear materials lying around. Where are you, Remo?"

"In the California desert. Ever hear of a Condome?"

"Yes. It's a new design in condominiums. A prototype is now under construction. I doubt they will catch on."

"Well, they caught Dirt First's attention. They were trying to nuke it for some reason, but we stopped them. We piled up a lot of bodies, Smitty."

"I will cover your tracks," Smith said in a tone of voice that said bodies were no more a problem than empty soda cans. "Have you found any proof that Dirt First!! was behind the La Plomo incident?"

"Nope. But I'd say we got them dead to rights." Remo's eyes went around the den. The knotty pine walls were lined with photos of Connors Swindell—usually breaking ground and wearing a hardhat that fit his beefy head like a thimble. Remo recognized several senators and other celebrities. One shot in particular drew his attention. The man standing arm in arm with Swindell looked familiar, but Remo couldn't place him. Probably a service buddy, he decided. He wore some kind of uniform.

"That is hardly proof," Smith pointed out.

"The FBI has determined that the L
Army surplus."

"That fits in with Chiun's theory tha
we found in Missouri was military. I stil
was a Dirt Firster."

"We should know soon. The FBI is processing the body. He is an annoying loose end. I would feel better if all the loose ends were tied together."

"What do you want—signed confessions? I'm an assassin, not Dale Cooper."

Smith sighed. "Very well. Return to Folcroft."

"As soon as we get the grand tour."

"Grand tour?"

"The developer is giving us a condo in return for services rendered."

"Do not accept it," Smith said sharply.

"Why not? I'll bet it's bug-free," Remo said pointedly.

Smith had no reply to that, so Remo disconnected, saying, "Chew on that a while, Smitty."

Remo found the Master of Sinanju in the bathroom examining the fixtures as Connors Swindell pointed out their attributes.

"You see this little doohickey here?" Swindell was saying, pointing to a gleaming stainless steel shower head.

"Yes. It is obviously a doohicky," Chiun said seriously.

"You just dial it and get any kind of water massage you want. Pulsing, throbbing, needle spray—you name it. Every home should have one."

"How about a quick tour before we go?" Remo asked.

"Your friend here is a hard sell," Swindell said, leading them out to the elevator. "Good thing I

...ody offered him a unit. I'd start to think I was losing my golden touch."

"The things you touch do not turn to gold," Chiun said coldly.

"Don't you just love this guy?" Swindell asks Remo. "He talks like an upscale fortune cookie!"

The elevator took them down into the Condome tower.

As they descended, the air became cooler, then clammier, and then finally dank with the smell of standing water.

"The air conditioner must have kicked back on," Remo remarked. "You could get Legionnaire's disease breathing this stuff."

"If you want the twenty-first-century luxury of living in the desert, you gotta make a few adjustments," Swindell said firmly.

"What do you think, Chiun?"

The Master of Sinanju did not answer at first. Remo wondered if he was being ignored again. Then he noticed Chiun's face. It was uneasy, the eyes a little strange.

The elevator stopped, and the doors slid open. Swindell stepped off. His feet sloshed with each step.

Remo looked out into the corridor warily. Connors Swindell, wearing a sheepish smile, was standing in a half inch of clammy water.

"Someone spill something?" Remo asked as Chiun sniffed the air unhappily.

"Those damn Dirt First!! saboteurs!" Swindell said indignantly. "Don't you fret. It's only a little water. This stuff will all be pumped out before you're ready to occupy."

Getting up on tiptoe, Remo stepped into the corridor.

He turned. "Coming, Little Father?"

The sheet-like look on the Master of Sinanju's face froze Remo's blood.

"Chiun! What's wrong?"

"Remo, we must leave this place of horror," Chiun said, his voice squeaking like rusty nails being pulled from dry wood.

"Horror?" Remo and Swindell said in unison. "What are you talking about?" Remo added, eyes concerned.

"Yeah," Swindell asked. "What the hell are you talking about?"

"This is a place of death," Chiun intoned. "Death and darkness. I refuse to enter it."

"But you got a unit just down the hall," Swindell protested. "Don't worry about a little water sloshing around the floor. It won't hurt you none."

"Remo," Chiun repeated, holding fast. "We must leave. Now."

It wasn't the edge in the Master of Sinanju's voice that decided Remo—although it grew more metallic and terrible in a way Chiun's voice had never before sounded—it was the soul-shocked light in his hazel eyes.

Remo wasted no time. He yanked Swindell back into the elevator with him and punched the up button.

"If you don't want it, at least tell your friends about it," Swindell said disspiritedly. "Fair enough?"

The elevator ride seemed to take twice as long going up as down. Once at the top, the Master of Sinanju fled the cage for the desert with a hurried padding of his sandals.

Chiun, Remo realized in surprise, was actually running from the Condome as if he feared it would somehow swallow him.

"What's eating your friend?" Swindell muttered. "Reverse acrophobia?"

"No idea," Remo said worriedly. He caught up with the Master of Sinanju. "Tell me what's wrong, Little Father?" he asked.

The Master of Sinanju slowed. He did not stop. He marched straight to the rental car. His hands found one another, clasping opposite wrists in the hidden folds of his kimono sleeves. Remo noticed that they trembled almost imperceptibly.

Chiun spoke in a hollow voice. "I smelled death, Remo. Terrible death. A long, black, clammy eternity of death. More grim than the Void from which we come and to which we return."

"I never heard you speak of death that way," Remo said. "Like you feared it."

"I do not fear a clean death," Chiun insisted. "A true and correct death is sometimes to be welcomed. The death that waits for me down in that buried place of horror is not such a death."

Remo lifted a eyebrow. "For you?"

"Come," Chiun said. "Take me away if you value the gifts I have bestowed upon you."

"Sure, Little Father," Remo said gently. "Just let me grab the neutron bomb pieces."

Chiun's head snapped around. His wrinkled face twisted in horror.

"Do what you must. But do not delay."

Remo hurried back to the wounded helicopter. He left the mangled casing rings and tucked the beryllium oxide tamper under one arm.

He ran back across the sand in such haste that he actually left footprints.

For once, the Master of of Sinanju declined to scold him on his carelessness.

They drove off in strained silence.

17

Remo was transcending with the sun.

It was an old Sinanju ritual. A Master of Sinanju would sit cross-legged on a reed mat, eyes closed, feeling the new sun beating on his face. As the sun rose, he would meditate on the events of the previous day and attempt to peer into those of the day to come.

In over twenty years of transcending with the sun, Remo had never seen a shred of the day to come. Today was no different.

He opened his eyes. The sun struck them like a double-bladed dagger. Straightening his crossed legs like an unfolding scissors jack, he came to his feet.

He turned, intending to see how Chiun was.

"Little Father!" he said, surprised. "I didn't know you were up."

For standing before him, his face a wrinkled blank, was the Master of Sinanju. He wore a pale peach-colored robe.

Chiun lifted a quelling hand.

"I have words to speak to you, Remo Williams," Chiun intoned.

"Well, pull up a mat," Remo said brightly.

Gravely the Master of Sinanju toed a tatami mat

into place. He settled onto it. Remo slipped back onto his. His hands settled on his lifted knees.

"I'm all ears," he said.

Remo half-expected a cutting rebuke. None came. Instead, Chiun began speaking in brittle tones. His eyes seemed unfocused as he talked, as if he were looking at something other than Remo. Remo shivered. Chiun's gaze bored through him and beyond, making Remo feel like a pane of glass. He had never felt that way. The glass was like a barrier, cutting him off from all contact with the man who had raised him up from common humanity.

"I had not expected to speak these words to you, my son," Chiun said hollowly. "But time is growing short."

Remo's brows knit together. "Short?"

"I am very old."

Uh-oh, thought Remo. Here we go again. Another I'm-in-my-last-days spiel. What's the old reprobate angling for this time?

"Tell me something new," Remo joked. The hazel eyes of the Master of Sinanju focused suddenly and Remo lost the transparent-as-glass feeling. Chiun's frank regard was devoid of warmth.

"I have seen many summers," Chiun began.

"I know," Remo said in a subdued voice. "You're what now? Eighty-something?"

"I was eighty when I first laid eyes upon you, white man with death in his heart."

"That's right. That makes you, what—over ninety?" Remo blinked at the realization. "Christ, where does the time go?"

"In all the years we have known one another, never have you acknowledged my birthday, never have you honored me for each year successfully completed. So it was last year. And the year before. So it would have been this very summer."

So that's it, Remo thought. Well, I got him there.

"Wait a darn minute here!" Remo said. "I never celebrated your birthday because you never let on when it was. In fact, I distinctly recall once asking, and being told to mind my own business."

"A truly worthy seeker of truth is not so easily dissuaded as that," Chiun said, his voice flint.

"Your exact words," Remo persisted, " 'Mind your own business, pale piece of pig's ear.' That was me in those days, a miserable pale piece of pig's ear."

"You have gained some color since those long-ago days," Chiun said without emotion. Remo tried to read the remark for humor. But Chiun had resumed speaking.

"In the land of my birth, Korea, men by custom cease to celebrate the days of their natural span with their sixtieth birthday. Their age is not acknowledged after that. To the end of their days, they remain eternally sixty."

"Kinda like a Korean thirty-nine," Remo remarked.

"But a Master of Sinanju is different," Chiun went on solemnly. "He celebrates his sixtieth year and his sixty-first and so on until he reaches the illustrious age of eighty."

"When *is* your birthday, anyway?" Remo asked suddenly. "I know you're a Leo. That's in what? June? July? A couple of months from now, at least."

"Beyond eighty," Chiun continued coldly, "a Master of Sinanju does not acknowledge the passing years until he reaches a certain milestone. This he acknowledges, and yet remains forever eighty. For it is an important event in a Master's life."

"Yeah?" Remo said, wondering where this was going.

"You wonder why I have shunned you of late?"

"It had crossed my mind," Remo said sourly. "Once or twice. Yeah."

"It had been my hope that you would come to this knowledge of your own accord."

"Sue me."

Chiun's button nose wrinkled in disdain.

Let him work for it, Remo thought. Two can play this game.

"Once," Chiun began, launching into the low, wavering tone he used to offer the legends of Sinanju, "the Master Songjong, who was young, being only sixty—"

"Is this a real sixty or a Korean thirty-nine?"

"Sixty by anyone's reckoning," Chiun said tartly. "Now, the Master who trained him, who was Vimu, was approaching the great milestone fortunate Masters reach. A summons came out of Egypt. It was a minor thing. Something about a princeling who lacked the patience to become a natural pharaoh. So he sought to slay the one who was ahead of him in the natural order."

"An old story," Remo noted.

"With the usual ending. And when word came to Vimu, he summoned Songjong and said to him, 'A summons has come out of Egypt. Since in these days Sinanju enjoys the luxury of two Masters to earn its gold, one of us must go to Egypt and the other remain to guard the gold earned in times past. Which do you prefer, my son?'

"And Master Songjong, who had been a good Master until now, meditated upon this. Instead of considering Vimu's age, he thought of a Korean maiden called Nari, with whom he was smitten. Being fifty, he had decided to take a wife. And he hoped to make this come to pass soon, for his loins burned with a lust for Nari."

"Late bloomer, huh?"

"And so did Songjong say unto the Master Vimu, 'O Master, you are old and approach the venerated age. The task in Egypt is modest, but the responsibility of guarding our village is great and must fall upon my shoulders in coming times. I should remain here now to perfect my skills of guardianship.'

"Vimu nodded gravely, although this was not the answer he had expected. The task would take him far from his ancestral village, and he would not return until after his coming birthday. Vimu was disappointed, since Songjong had knowledge of this fact, but he surrendered to the decision. For Vimu had placed the matter before Songjong as a test of his competence. And while Songjong had failed, it still remained for Vimu to go to Egypt."

Chiun's voice fell into a mournful singsong cadence.

"With much heartache, Master Vimu ventured into the sands of Egypt. The princeling was dispatched as easily as most princelings are. But saddened and advanced in age, Master Vimu did not survive the long journey back through the dark desert. He died, parched of tongue, and his skin hardened to iron."

Chiun raised an ivory-nailed finger.

"One day short of his hundredth birthday."

"Tough," said Remo carelessly. Then it sank in. "Wait a minute! Did you say hundred? That's the venerated age?"

Chiun nodded gravely.

Remo pointed to Chiun's sunken breast.

"You! You're a hundred!"

Chiun shook his aged head. "I beheld my ninety-ninth summer last year. This summer, if I live to see it, I will attain the venerated age all Masters strive for, for it means that they have completed their mission in life. For ever since the days of Songjong and Vimu, it has been decreed that upon attaining the exalted age, a Master of Sinanju may retire if he so desires."

"Are you telling me you're planning to retire?"

"No, ignorant one," said Chiun. "I am telling you this for two reasons. The first is that you are obviously too blind to discover the truth for yourself, as I had hoped. And there are great ceremonies which are your responsibility to initiate."

"What's the second?"

Chiun rose. His face was like beige stone weathered by a thousand years of wind and rain. His eyes were bleak and animal sad.

"The second reason is that I do not believe I will attain the venerated age."

And with those words the Master of Sinanju whirled and returned to his room. The door closed quietly. Remo stared at it a long time. But he wasn't looking at the wood. Remo Williams was seeing the afterimage of Chiun's stooped figure in his mind's eye. It was as if he beheld the Master of Sinanju's true frailty for the first time.

"A hundred years old," Remo whispered. "He's a hundred freaking years old."

He felt a cold wind blow through the room, even though it was a warm spring day.

A shiver rippled along the bare skin of his forearms.

18

Connors Swindell's decade was taking a turn for the worse.

It was the next morning. His secretary, seeing the ashen look on his usually flush-with-prospects face as he entered his Palm Springs condo, accidentally pricked herself with the needle she was busily wielding.

"Ouch!" she said, sucking on her thumb. She threw down the needle and tossed the now-blood-stained condom into the wastebasket, saying. "That one's no good now."

"That's what I want," Connors said savagely. "You fetch it back, hear?"

Reluctantly Connie Payne fished the rolled-up condom from the basket, and wetting a Kleenex with her tongue, wiped the blood off. Then, after holding it up to the light to make sure the pinhole went clean through the lambskin, she slipped it into the slot of a small device on her desk that resembled a high-tech stamping machine. As she tapped the lever, the device hissed and spat out the condom, now sealed in foil stamped with the name Connors Swindell on one side. The other side held a strip of Velcro. She affixed the packet to a similarly Velcroed búsiness card and flipped it onto a growing pile.

As she unwrapped another condom from its fresh-from-the-factory packet, Connie looked up at her employer.

"You know, I could be doing this for years," she complained.

"I pay you," Swindell said, stripping off his jacket and hanging it on a peg. "And you might as well be doing something as sitting on your pretty little butt. We ain't moving units like the old days, you know."

"I heard about those Dirt First people on the radio. Are they all dead?"

"What ain't road kill is. They messed up my Condome but good. Insurance don't cover this. We may have to cash out."

"What about all that Missouri property you were going to buy? Can't we stall the creditors until they come on the market, Con honey?"

"How many times I gotta tell you? Don't 'Con honey' me. It ain't professional. In bed you can 'Con honey' me all you like. No place else."

"Sorry *Mr.* Swindell," Connie said frostily, piercing the condom and feeding it through the stamper. Another packet clicked into the pile.

"That's better, but don't skimp on the warmth."

"This is a long way to go to start another baby boom." She pouted. "I'll be a saggy old lady by then."

"You always got a stall in my stable, you know that," Swindell said absently, looking through the stack of letters on his secretary's desk. "Anything special in here?" he asked.

"The one on top's another paternity suit."

Swindell dropped the envelope into the wastebasket. "Nobody wants to pay the piper no more," he muttered.

"The electric and phone bills are both overdue."

"So? Draw two checks."

"Against what? We're tapped."

"Do it anyway. Just make sure you stick the phone check in the electric envelope and vice versa. That oughta tangle up their shorts for another three weeks."

"Oh, Con. You're such a genius," Connie said admiringly.

"If I'm so smart, how come I'm in so much debt?"

"Maybe you should pay more attention to your horoscope, like I told you to."

Swindell grunted. He dropped the remaining mail into the wastebasket. "Taggert call yet?"

"Not yet."

"If anybody wanting to buy calls," Connors Swindell said wearily, "I'll be in my office. I'm out to salesmen, lawyers, and creditors."

The door slammed sullenly, and Constance Payne went back to putting pinholes in condoms. It was boring work, but every time she passed a newborn in a stroller, it gave her a tiny swell of pride. Who knew how many newborns owed their lives to the most brilliant real-estate-promotion scheme in human history?

In the sunshine-filled sanctity of his Palm Springs den, Connors Swindell didn't feel at all brilliant. He felt instead like he was drowning in warm air.

This latest setback to the Condome development looked to be a mortal blow. The banks would be all over him when they got the news that Dirt First!! had trashed the site. He had spent the entire night trying to clean it up, but it was useless.

"Damn those ecobusybodies!" he burst out. "Imagine them messing with my plans twice."

The phone rang. Swindell scooped it up.

"Mr. Taggert on line one," Connie chimed.

"Put 'im through." A moment later: "Hello, Taggert? About time you got back to me."

"I don't appreciate your tone," said a voice that sounded like Humphrey Bogart in a dry well.

"Sorry. I'm having a bad decade. Listen, the reason I called yesterday is, I got another special job for you."

"Yeah?"

"The La Plomo thing is fixing to work out fine," Swindell said. "I aim to scoop up all them fine houses—the ones still standing, that is—real cheap, just like I planned."

"Don't forget I get first choice."

"Glad you mentioned that," Swindell said breathily, leaning into the phone. "I saw the cutest French Colonial you ever did see. You like it, it's yours."

"Don't forget my Condome unit too. When do I get the tour?"

"Soon, soon," Swindell said vaguely. "I got a great bottom-floor unit with your name on the door. You can see it as soon as we pump—"

"Pump?"

"I mean finish it off. Now, listen. Taggert, you can find anything, right?"

"I found you all that poison gas."

"That you did. Listen. I had me a kinda setback. I lost something mighty valuable to me."

"Describe the item."

"Spoken like a true private detective, which you are," said Swindell heartily. "But the item I have in mind got damaged. It's no good to me anymore. I need another."

"So what is this item?"

Swindell swiveled in his chair. Beyond the window, stands of twisted Joshua trees rippled magically. They repeated in a nearby wall-length mirror, a nice touch, he thought.

"A neutron bomb," Connors Swindell said softly.

"Are you crazy? What do you want with a neutron bomb?"

"Same thing I wanted with all that damn gas. To shake some dinks loose of their prime real estate. You know, there's lots of folks holding on to property these days instead of trading up and fueling the real-estate sector of the economy. It's downright un-American."

"I was lucky to find the gas. A neutron bomb may be out of my league."

"Probably. But a tall hank of a hippie girl ain't."

"Come again?"

"There's this girl name of Sky Bluel. Must come from a long line of hippies or something with a name like that. She built a bomb. I ended up with it, but the CIA took it away from me."

"CIA!" Taggert exploded. "Christ, Swindell, what if this line is bugged? We'll both be doing federal time in Atlanta."

"No chance. The CIA blamed those Dirt Firsters. They happened to be in two inconvenient places in one day, like they was following me. Not that they were. The thing of it is, I got hold of their neutron bomb and they got the blame."

"That's convenient."

"But then one of them jerks stole my helicopter, which had the bomb in it. Crashed it good. I lost the bomb and the helicopter both."

"You're lucky to be alive."

Connors Swindell examined his pinkie diamond ring. He blew on it.

"Naw. Bomb didn't have a core."

"What good was it, then?"

"Reason I called you in the first place was, I wanted you to scrounge me up a core."

"Somehow, I don't think 'scrounge' is quite the word for it," Taggert said dryly.

"Never mind that. Look, you find this Sky Bluel. Kidnap her and I'll have her build me a new neutron bomb. It'll be better than poison gas."

"What do you have in mind?"

"I was kinda thinking of clearing those filthy-rich snowbirds outta Orlando and snapping up what the heirs don't get, just like I'm trying to do in La Plomo."

"If you nuke Orlando, Florida, I guarantee you the heirs will sell out to you for ten cents on the dollar."

"I figure a nickel. Times are tough. I can't afford ten. Then I'm gonna rename the place Swindellburg. Catchy, huh?"

"That's your business," Taggert said flatly. "What's in it for me?"

"I got this here industrial park just sitting out in New Jersey, on the banks of the Hudson, without any tenants," Swindell said, thinking of a property he had acquired in boom times, unaware the ground was contaminated with PCB's. "I'll sign title over to you. And you do with it what you want—rent, sublease, subdivide, name your poison."

"Sounds fair. You know, this is better than taking cash."

"It's called trading up, and it's how I made my empire."

"So where do I find Sky Bluel?"

"She made the news the other night. That's your lead."

"Got it. One last thing."

Swindell smiled into the phone. With his free hand he eased a silver Waterman pen from his inner jacket pocket.

"You're about to ask me about poor, departed Horace Feely," he suggested smoothly.

"Departed?"

"He helped me with the bomb, just like he did my dirty work buyin' all that poison gas. Which is more than I can say for some."

"You hired me to find, not acquire. That's why I only charged a finder's fee."

Swindell fingered the cap off the pen. Instead of a nib, a slim hollow-nosed needle gleamed in its place. And in the clear reservoir tube, a vile yellow liquid sloshed.

"So anyway," he said absently, "seein' as how he was makin' blackmail noises, I gave him a little squirt of gas. Got me a pen tricked out to deliver it. I just shoved that sucker up the other sucker's nostril and gave him what-for. Answer your question?"

"It does."

The line went dead.

Connors Swindell hung up the phone. He exhaled a hot breath. This was getting deeper. First murder, then dealing in nukes, now kidnapping, but if he was going to survive the real-estate slump of the nineties, he had to take steps.

And hell, it wasn't that much worse than some of the things he had pulled in his used-car days, rolling back odometers and selling cars with defective brakes. A few more folks died, was all.

He capped his custom Waterman and returned it to his inside jacket pocket. He was down to his last squirt of Lewisite. No telling when he might have to fall back on it.

19

Don Cooder entered the network studio in lower Manhattan wearing the same unflinching expression that stared down ninety million American TV viewers each weeknight at seven o'clock—six-thirty central time.

The program director met him, waving a sheaf of papers and shouting at the top of his lungs.

"Don! Where on earth have you been? The brass want to know what's going on with tonight's *Twenty-four Hours* installment, and I don't know what to tell them."

"Tell them," Don Cooder said forcefully, "we're working on the most explosive edition ever."

"But the promos!" the program director moaned, hurrying after him. "We don't have any promos to air!"

"That's what I came down for," Cooder bit out.

"What about the script?"

"No script. It's all live, all spontaneous, in the Don Cooder tradition."

That comment stopped the program director in his tracks. Although the highest-paid anchor in the business, Don Cooder was not renowned for his smooth extemporaneous delivery. In fact, without a script his demeanor was closer to that of a pregnant bride walking down the aisle.

Visions of sixty minutes of impending prime-time disaster flashed through his mind as he followed Cooder to the familiar *Evening News with Don Cooder* set. Cooder signaled a cameraman and the set became active. Lights blazed. Cameras dollied in.

Cooder marched over to a stool and perched on it. He was into stools this year, his previous attempt to be different—standing before a global map like a wrapped-too-tight geography teacher—had flopped worse than the much-ridiculed sweater-vest gimmick.

Taking a deep breath, the program director threw him a cue. The red light went on. Don Cooder gave the camera lens a challenging look.

"Tonight on *Twenty-four Hours*," he intoned, "you will see, live for the first time on network television, an armed neutron bomb capable of obliterating New York City. And, too, you will meet the high-school girl who built it. Are our high-school students building deadly nuclear devices under our very noses? The answers tonight, on *Twenty-four Hours*. Be there. Or be square."

The program director wore shock on his face like baby powder.

"Don," he gasped. "Say it's a joke. Please, Don. I know you don't have a sense of humor, but lie if you have to."

"Don Cooder never jokes," Don Cooder growled. Without another word, he left the studio and the building, confident that by the next rating book he would be the top network anchor in the universe.

The *Twenty-four Hours* promotion was aired four times that day. Twice during the local evening news, once during the *Evening News with Don*

Cooder, and again in the dead half-hour before local programming gave way to eight o'clock and the start of prime time.

All across the nation, millions of people saw that promo.

Calvin Taggert, in a New York bar, where he had followed an intricate trail to Sky Bluel's current whereabouts, was the first. Unable to locate Bluel, Taggert had bugged her parents' telephone. From the cryptic twice-daily calls the girl had made, he figured out she was somewhere in Manhattan. So he had caught the red-eye and hit the bricks.

Sky Bluel had let slip something about a very important national TV news appearance. Taggert swiftly cased the various network headquarters buildings without result. So he had repaired to a bar for a quick J&B on the rocks before resuming the search.

There Don Cooder's hard-bitten voice jumped out of the bar TV like a western gunfighter calling on an owlhoot to draw.

"There is a God," Taggert breathed, finishing his drink in a gulp. Slapping down a generous tip, he rushed outside to hail a cab.

Barry Kranish, sipping a jagua-juice cocktail after his second visit to his urologist, also caught the promo.

He lay in bed, propped up with five pillows—sore from the flexible scope the urologist had burrowed into his tender urethra in a futile search for bloodsucking catfish—and watched local news recaps of the decimation of Dirt First!!

The urologist, who had assured Kranish there were no *candiru* lurking in his gallbladder, had prescribed two Valium and a month's rest.

"I am not overworked," Kranish had protested.

"Once these *candiru* get into the gallbladder, there's almost no way to dislodge them. I don't want to end up as a catfish's last meal. The rain forest needs me."

"I can understand your concern," the doctor said soothingly. "Your fine organization decimated, naturally you'd be depressed, overwrought. Take the Valium."

"I only use natural antidepressants," Kranish spat, storming out. He bought a five-gallon can of double-chocolate ice cream on the way home.

As he watched TV, licking chocolate off a natural wood spoon, he wondered why his mood hadn't improved. Chocolate had never failed him before. Maybe it was artificial.

Kranish perked up at the stentorian blare of the *Twenty-four Hours* promo. He had always liked Don Cooder, especially after he had saved the humpback whale. Too bad the guy came across as such a stiff, always trying to sound hip when he wasn't.

Kranish absorbed the promo in stony silence. When it was over, he looked like a poster boy for the genetically stunned.

His mouth opened. "Neutron bomb?" he croaked.

His mind went back to the events of the last five days. The attack by those crazed would-be infiltrators. He knew now they were government plants. Even if the Asian one didn't exactly affect the button-down look. But the skinny guy had had pig written all over him.

That experience was shocking enough, but when the FBI later showed up at his door, spattered with pigeon guano, demanding to know about the Dirt First!! protest at Connors Swindell's Condome construction site, Kranish angrily got into the agents' collective faces.

"I happen to be Dirt First's legal counsel," he had told them indignantly. "And I deny any specific knowledge of any organized Dirt First!! protests. And even if I did, I claim client confidentiality. So just tell me where I go to bail them out."

"The morgue," he was told. The oinker FBI agent seemed almost pleased to relay the terrible news.

Woodenly Barry Kranish had gone to the morgue. He emerged shaking with the realization that he was a general without soldiers. And all—at least if the FBI could be believed—because the noble ecowarriors of Dirt First!! had attempted to save the oppressed desert scorpion and its precious abode.

After bailing himself out, Barry Kranish had returned to Dirt First!! headquarters and his private digs to avenge their deaths.

He had had no idea how to pursue vengeance. He was, after all, kind of a mellow guy. Managing finances was more in his line.

But as he watched the *Twenty-four Hours* promo, it all came together. Whatever had gone awry, it all started with that upstart girl Sky Bluel and her environmentally reckless neutron bomb. Kranish knew all about the horrors of the neutron bomb. He had voted for Jimmy Carter. Twice.

A plan began to form in his mind. One that would avenge his fallen comrade, protect the scorpion, and reclaim the desert from selfish, sand-disturbing, encroaching humanity.

Leaping out of bed, Barry Kranish hopped into his jeans. He left the tub of double chocolate melting on the bedclothes.

Let the bull cockroaches have it, he thought. They deserved some happiness too. Bless their endangered little feelers. Someday, after they had inherited the planet from doomed humankind, they would remember him.

Dr. Harold W. Smith had the soul of an accountant.

He believed in a place for every paper clip, and every paper clip in its place. He swore by the bottom line. "Two plus two equals four" was an article of faith with him. These were just the least of the reasons a young President had, many years ago, selected him to head CURE.

Frowning before his Folcroft computer, Smith realized things were not adding up.

It had been five days since Remo and Chiun had returned from California with the harmless beryllium-oxide tamper. The FBI investigation of Dirt First!! had continued to progress slowly.

Backtracking to La Plomo, they had taken possession of the half-naked corpse found beside Sky Bluel's pickup truck, with its puzzling headband imprint.

The official autopsy report had come in. According to an FBI forensics team, the still-unidentified man had been killed by a tiny but lethal exposure to Lewisite—the same deadly gas that had killed the inhabitants of La Plomo, Missouri. Oddly, only one lung was affected. But it had been enough.

Yet the time of death had been several weeks after the La Plomo incident. The very day Remo had found the body, in fact.

It was a troubling anomaly, Smith decided. It meant the architects of the La Plomo massacre had not exhausted their poison-gas supply, as Smith had assumed. And hoped.

Why, then, had Dirt First!! gone to such lengths to acquire a neutron bomb? And why had they taken it, of all places, to the Condome construction site?

Smith had done a background check of the Condome project. He uncovered very little he had not already read in the papers. The papers were full of the project, which had been greeted with general derision as the crackpot scheme of a desperate developer.

Connors Swindell was very close to bankruptcy, Smith learned after infiltrating the bank computer records of his primary lender. Sixty days away from default at the very most. And Connors Swindell had been personally besieged by countless lawsuits. Their exact nature was unclear. Probably environmental-impact nuisance suits, he decided.

This much did add up. A stop-work decree was imminent. The Condome project was doomed.

So why had Dirt First targeted Swindell? Smith wondered once more. The question nagged him.

It was still nagging him when the call came in from Reno.

"Smitty, I think we have trouble."

"What's this?" Smith asked.

"I have the TV on right now. Listen to this."

Over the phone Harold Smith heard the tinny voice of Don Cooder babbling about a live neutron bomb. That was all he needed to hear.

"Remo, come back," Smith said urgently. "Explain this."

"Remember Sky Bluel?" Remo asked.

"Of course. I have had the FBI looking for her all week."

"They should watch more TV. She's going to be on *Twenty-four Hours* tonight, showing off her latest toy. She built another one, Smitty."

"Disturbing, but not critical. The last one had no core."

"According to Cooder, this one is live and he's gonna broadcast it live. Everyone knows the guy's desperate for ratings. He might just detonate it, too."

"Preposterous, Remo. But for the good of the country, Sky Bluel must not go on the air tonight."

"I'll get on it," Remo said. "I thought this assignment was all over with. I just hope Swindell doesn't show up again."

"Connors Swindell?" Smith inquired. "Why would he?"

"Well, he was at La Plomo and again at the Condome site."

Smith's voice became sharp and tangy. "Remo. You never told me you met Connors Swindell in Missouri."

"Sure, I did. He was the condom salesman who talked like a realtor. I mentioned him."

"Not by name."

"Pardon me for losing my scorecard," Remo said acidly. "This hasn't exactly been an uncomplicated assignment."

"What was Swindell doing at La Plomo?"

"I think he saw it as a chance to make a big killing, real-estate-wise."

"How odd," Smith said slowly.

"I don't think so. He goes to Missouri to grab some bargains. Dirt First!! was there, too. They get upstaged by Sky Bluel and her traveling nuclear device, and since Swindell was throwing his business cards in everyone's face, they get the idea to give him some grief. Kinda like a consolation prize. It fits."

"Possibly," Smith said distantly. "Remo, take charge of Sky Bluel and the device. I will work on other scenarios."

"What other scenarios? I solved the mystery. End of story."

"Later," Smith said, hanging up. He returned to his computer.

A new anomaly had been introduced into the equation. Whether it would cause the equation to balance or force Smith to rewrite the entire formula depended on what else his computers unearthed on Connors Swindell.

In his Rye, New York, home, Remo Williams hung up the telephone.

He padded over to the big-screen TV before which the Master of Sinanju sat, eating cold rice from a wooden bowl and watching a taped British soap opera. He wore a royal purple kimono.

"Smith wants me to collect Sky Bluel and her latest bomb before New York is turned into a ghost town," Remo said solicitously. Then he made one of the most costly mistakes of his life. "Why don't you just sit this one out? Until you're feeling better?"

The Master of Sinanju tapped the remote control. The picture froze, flickering in distortion.

His trembling head swiveled toward Remo. "Do you think that because I am approaching the venerated age, I have grown too infirm to accompany you on Emperor Smith's business?"

"It's not that," Remo protested. "It's just that you've been moping around the house ever since we got back from California. I don't think you're in the best frame of mind to—"

"Do not lie to me, Remo Williams. I know only too well how whites treat their aged. They hide them in terrible homes, as if ashamed of those who gave them life. I will not be so treated. No tiresome home will be my fate."

"Retirement," Remo corrected. "Retirement home."

"No retirement home will be my fate," Chiun repeated, coming to his feet like uncoiling colored smoke. "I will accompany you."

"Age before beauty," Remo said jokingly, bowing so Chiun could precede him out the front door.

The Master of Sinanju slammed the door after him so hard Remo couldn't get it open again and, cursing himself, had to exit the house through a window.

20

Sky Bluel couldn't make up her mind.

Should she wear the fringed buckskin jacket over torn blue jeans or go for the peasant-blouse look?

The limousine was due any minute. Her latest neutron bomb sat in the bathroom, every shaped plastique charge in place and locked so no one could mess with it. She wore the only key around her neck. Without it, the bomb could not be neutralized. But her thoughts weren't on the bomb, which was almost twice the size of the previous device. Instead, Sky tried to decide what kind of statement she wanted to make. Fringed buckskin evoked the sixties of draft-card-burning. The peasant blouse was more Age of Aquarius sixties. Not nearly radical enough.

She modeled the buckskin in front of the full-length bathroom-door mirror, humming the theme from *Hair* and looking forward to leaving the hotel. Even if it was for a stuffy TV studio.

Finally she decided to go with the buckskin. That important choice made, the only remaining question was whether to go with body paint or a copper peace symbol mounted on a rawhide headband. Body paint seemed tacky, but maybe it would take the edge off the buckskin.

* * *

Barry Kranish had it narrowed down to the white limousine idling in front of the network building or the black limousine parked around back.

He knew Sky Bluel was not in the building itself. Kranish had found this out in a most direct manner. He had walked up to the main-entrance guard, flashed his business card, and announced he had a subpoena for Sky Bluel.

"And unless your network wants to be slapped with a lawsuit for obstruction of justice," he had said darkly, "somebody had better produce her." For effect, he waved his rental-car agreement under the guard's nose. There was no subpoena.

The desk guard summoned the head of security, who in turn called down a network vice-president.

"The person you are seeking is not in the building," the vice-president informed him stiffly. "At present."

"Where is she, then?" Kranish had demanded.

"I can't reveal that without jeopardizing the First Amendment rights of the press and possibly toppling the republic."

"This is not over," Kranish warned, storming from the building. On his way out, he bumped into a casually dressed man loitering by the door.

"Excuse me," the man said in a tone that carried no apology.

"Shove it," Kranish said, brushing past the man. He had security written all over him. Or maybe private heat. The coplike eyes and thick-soled brogans were dead giveaways.

The fact that the man abruptly stubbed out his cigarette and left the building a few paces behind him clinched it.

Barry Kranish had not gotten the answer he'd hoped for, but he had gotten the one he expected.

Sky Bluel was not in the building. That only meant that she soon would be.

As he waited in his rental car on the busy Manhattan street, Kranish decided on the white limousine. The liveried chauffeur at the wheel looked impatient. He was probably waiting to be told where to pick up the girl. So he settled down to wait. He noticed the private security guard now loitering by the studio entrance, smoking casually and eyeing both the idling limo and Barry Kranish with shifty half-intelligent eyes.

Kranish decided to keep his eye on him too. No telling where he might fit in when things started happening. Not that he was worried about a private dick. He had hired enough of them to get dirt on his political enemies to understand the breed.

Calvin Taggert sucked down a hot cloud of smoke and blew it out one nostril, paused, and then emptied his lungs through the other. It was a trick he had learned watching forties movies.

It was a good break, he decided, that he had overheard that lawyer pump the front guard about Sky Bluel. After repeated attempts to buy off assorted security and maintenance people, he had come up with nothing. Time was wasting. Once the girl got on TV, she would become the focus of every reporter from here to Alaska, and a thousand times harder to snatch.

He figured the white limousine idling by the door was there to pick her up.

So he settled down to wait, noticing that the lawyer was up to the same thing. But Calvin Taggert wasn't worried about the lawyer. Still, he would keep an eye on him too. His eyes looked a little feverish, like he was on drugs or something.

* * *

When it came, the break he had hoped for practically stepped up and shook Calvin Taggert's hand.

It was twenty minutes to eight, twenty minutes to air time for *Twenty-four Hours*. He was starting to wonder if he should check the back when Don Cooder himself emerged from the studio building and stepped up to the chauffeur, who sat patiently behind the wheel.

"Okay," he said, leaning down to speak in the chauffeur's ear, "it's the Penta. Go get her."

Cooder gave the roof an urgent slap, and the limousine pulled away from the curb.

Calvin Taggert raced to his rental car and threw himself behind the wheel. He cut off a Federal Express truck and sideswiped a taxi getting the car into the flow of traffic. Despite this, he managed to position himself only three car lengths behind the limousine. He spotted the lawyer's car jockeying behind the limo. That didn't worry him. What was a lawyer going to do? Threaten him with the sharp edge of a subpoena?

Sky Bluel had just finished daubing a passion-purple peace symbol on her right cheek when the hotel-room phone rang.

It was the front desk. "Your driver is here, miss."

"Fab, send him up," Sky said, closing her paintbox. The daisy she intended to adorn the tip of her nose would have to await a better time.

The man who buzzed was not a chauffeur, Sky saw as she opened the door. Instead of a chauffeur's uniform, or even a suit, he wore green work pants and a jersey.

"You're my driver?" she said doubtfully.

"Not me," the man rumbled. "I'm a studio stagehand. The driver's downstairs." His gorillalike arms dangled loose at his sides. He looked like a dock-worker, not a TV person, Sky thought.

"I guess you get to carry my pride and joy," Sky said, stepping aside. "It's in the tub."

"Thanks." The big guy lumbered into the bathroom, where he found the neutron device balanced across the porcelain rim. Wrapping huge paws around either end of the electronics-studded breadboard mounting, he lifted it straight up.

Carrying it like an oversize serving dish, he duck-walked out into the corridor.

"What the hell is this thing?" he complained as Sky closed the door behind them.

"It's a neutron bomb, okay? So don't drop it."

"You have my solemn word on that," he said in a thin voice.

As the elevator descended, Sky Bluel had stars in her eyes. She had stars on her face too, but she absently scratched her chin and obliterated both of them.

After tonight, she thought, a whole generation would march behind her, in lockstep, into the future.

"You remember the sixties?" she asked excitedly.

"Not me. I lived through them."

"Well, the sixties are coming back, and I'm going to be the next Jane Fonda. Isn't that absolutely boss?"

The studio worker stifled a laugh. Sky frowned. Maybe "boss" was more fifties slang. She would have to ask her father when she got home.

There were no parking spaces.

"Damn!" Calvin Taggert said bitterly, circling the block with reckless disregard for pedestrians. The white limo was still outside the Penta Hotel, still idling, still empty. But time was running out. He would have to start making moves soon or he could kiss that nice Missouri retirement home good-bye.

He passed the lawyer's car. The lawyer was a real amateur. He was staring out the windshield, craning his head to keep the hotel entrance in sight. For some strange reason, he had smeared his face with brown jungle camouflage paint or something. He was so obvious, he might as well have worn a neon cowbell.

Taggert flipped him the finger in passing.

Barry Kranish clutched the steering wheel in a brown-knuckled death grip. His knuckles were brown because that was the color of the river mud he had plunged them into before slapping his face into a ball of unrecognizable gunk. In his heart he swelled with newfound respect for his fallen Dirt First!! comrades. For one thing, the smell would make a maggot puke.

Guerrilla ectotage was scarier than he'd thought. He wondered what would happen to him if he were captured. Who would bail him out? Maybe he would be forced to defend himself. He shivered.

While he was turning the dire possibilities over in his mind, the hotel's massive revolving door started to turn.

Kranish reached for the car-door lever. Then the girl stepped out, looking like a walking LSD flashback, followed by the liveried chauffeur.

"The bomb!" Kranish moaned, pounding the steering wheel. "Where's the damn bomb?"

Calvin Taggert turned the corner and his heart leapt up into his throat, forcing a curse out ahead of it.

"Shit! There she is."

He looked frantically for a parking slot. Since the

hotel faced Madison Square Garden and Pennsylvania Station, parking was almost impossible. He sent the car around for a final pass. The girl was walking to the limo now. Once she got inside, it would be infinitely harder to nail her.

Then the side door opened and a beefy man carrying an oversize electronic device backed out. Clumsily he turned around and almost lost his balance. His face went white.

"Be careful!" Sky Bluel shouted. "Don't break it! You'll ruin everything!"

The chauffeur came to the rescue. He leapt to the other man's side and lent a supporting hand.

"Okay, I got it," the beefy man said, gingerly lugging the device to the open trunk of the waiting limousine.

"Looks like it's now or never," Taggert muttered, pulling a rayon stocking over his head.

When the neutron bomb almost slipped from the beefy guy's hands, Barry Kranish made his move. Dripping mud, he plunged from the car carrying a railroad spike by its pointed end. He lifted it high.

Then a car suddenly screeched out of traffic and lunged up on the wide sidewalk, heading right for the chauffeur.

"Stop!" the chauffeur bleated.

The car didn't stop.

Before he knew what had hit him, the car grille picked up the chauffeur and carried him right into the unyielding hotel facade. He bounced off and his upper body landed on the hood, broken legs pinned between the bumper and the building.

Sky Bluel screamed. She called to the beefy stagehand from the studio.

"Don't just stand there, do something!"

No answer. She tore her eyes away from the body and looked back.

The beefy guy lay sprawled on the sidewalk, his head spurting red fluid like a spasmodic squirt gun.

"God, this is worse than Kent State!" she moaned.

Another man had the neutron bomb, Sky saw to her mounting horror. Holding one end up by both hands, he was dragging the board along the side-walk. There was mud everywhere.

"Stop! That's my bomb. What are you doing with my bomb?"

"Get a generation," the man called back, spitting brown droplets.

Desperate, Sky Bluel looked around for help. A man in a rumpled suit stepped from the car that had pinned the chauffeur. He looked like some kind of plainclothes cop, so Sky swallowed her pride and said, "See that man? That's my property he's stealing."

"Too bad," the man said in a cold voice. He was balling a handkerchief up in one hand. The other held a clear bottle, which he unscrewed with the flick of a strong thumb.

Looking fierce, the man capped the bottle with the cloth and upended it. It reminded Sky of old movies where the bad guy would chloroform an intended victim. They were pre-sixties movies and the women always acted helpless and screamed. It was too regressive for words, so Sky had always changed the channel at those parts. Consequently, she had no idea how to react now.

She decided to run. Too late.

The man caught her by the braided rawhide thong around her neck. The handkerchief jammed into her mouth and nose and the smell was like a really bad trip. Although the colors were interesting.

Sky Bluel fought the mounting odor that filled her lungs. She clutched at the strong hand. It might as well have been stone. Struggling, she snapped the rawhide thong, but by then it was too late. Far too late.

Sky was unconscious before the man gathered her up in his arms and threw her into the passenger seat of his car. He slid behind the wheel. The car backed up, hurling the dead chauffeur to the sidewalk, where he sustained several posthumous contusions, and vanished in traffic.

It went north. The car being driven by Barry Kranish went west. When the police arrived several minutes later, the overlapping descriptions of the fleeing cars they got from passersby tied them up a solid hour while they sorted it all out.

By the time they realized they were dealing with two separate assailants driving two different cars, the trail had gotten too cold to pick up.

When Don Cooder received the news from the pair of stone-faced police officers that not only had he no neutron bomb to stun the nation on tonight's *Twenty-four Hours*, but also his featured guest, Sky Bluel, had been abducted, he did not flinch.

He told the two police officers who had come to question him, "Could you excuse me for a moment, please?" and went into his office.

Twenty minutes later, the impatient police barged in.

They found Don Cooder hiding under his desk, a shell-shocked expression on his face, repeating something unintelligible over and over in a thick voice. He was unintelligible because he had his thumb in his mouth.

"What's that he's saying?" one cop asked the other.

"Sounds like 'What's the frequency, Kenneth?' "

"Sounds like we came to the wrong place," Remo whispered to Chiun as he absorbed the police account of the double abduction.

"There are more wrong places than this," Chiun said coldly.

They had been at the studio more than an hour. After slipping into the building and ascertaining that Sky Bluel was not there, they had decided to wait in the concealment of a darkened morning-show set.

The arrival of the police and the commotion that followed—particularly the anguished cries of a program director when he realized he had neither star, nor guest, nor material for the evening broadcast of *Twenty-four Hours*—made them realize something had gone wrong.

"What is the meaning of 'What is the frequency, Kenneth?' " Chiun asked as they exited the studio unseen.

"One of the two early-warning signs of an impending nervous breakdown," Remo explained.

"And what is the other?"

"Finding yourself dead last in the ratings."

They went immediately to the Penta entrance, which was only then being cordoned off with yellow police-barrier tape.

There they mingled with the crowd, picking up snatches of overheard exchanges between newly arrived detectives and witnesses. A detective was dropping a rawhide cord into a clear evidence bag.

"Sounds like they got Sky and the bomb," Remo muttered.

"Who are 'they'?" Chiun asked darkly.

"Damned if I know," Remo spat. "Maybe Cooder set this up. Anything is possible with that guy."

"This is obviously the handiwork of the same perpetrators as before," Chiun said, regarding the sprawled bodies. Both were draped by sheets, except that the head of one had been uncovered by a medical examiner for the benefit of a morgue photographer.

"How?" Remo said. "The Dirt Firsters all bit the dirt—so to speak. Except that screwball lawyer, Kranish. And this isn't his style. It must have been someone else. Terrorists who saw the news promo, or the Dirt Firsters' military connection."

"Behold that dead man, Remo," Chiun intoned, indicating the body with the exposed face. "Does he not remind you of someone?"

Remo looked. "No"

"Look closer. At his forehead."

Remo did. He saw a faint line circling the man's brow.

"Hey! Just like the dead guy we found in Missouri. See, Chiun? That proves it. He was a Dirt Firster. He musta lost his headband when he got run over."

"Then whose cap is that?" Chiun asked pointedly.

Remo followed Chiun's pointing finger. He saw the plain brown cap lying crushed on the sidewalk.

"Is that a military cap?" he asked.

"I do not think so. There is no insignia."

"I gotta check this out," Remo said, stepping over the police-barrier tape.

None of the detectives noticed him as he picked up the cap and stepped up to the corpse. The morgue photographer had gone over to the other body.

"Excuse me, pal," Remo told the corpse politely, whipping the sheet away. His eyes blinked at the sight of a chauffeur's brown livery. "Chauffeur?" he muttered blankly. To be sure, he lifted the man's inert head and tried out the cap. It was a perfect fit.

"Damn," Remo muttered, standing up. "A freaking chauffeur."

That got him noticed by the police.

"Hey! Who the hell are you?" the plainclothes detective with the evidence bag demanded.

"FBI," Remo said, offering a card from his wallet.

"This card says you're an EPA investigator," the detective said belligerently, "and I say you're under arrest."

"You got me," Remo said, offering his thick wrists.

The detective reached into his coat for his handcuffs. Somehow he got tangled up and found himself on the sidewalk, his left wrist cuffed to his right ankle.

He called for help, but the crime-scene team were all busy chasing his thick-wristed attacker into the crowd.

Later, when they returned empty-handed, wearing hangdog expressions, they were in no mood to add the incident to their official reports.

Once the detective had been freed of his own handcuffs, they put it to a vote. The decision was unanimous.

They never saw any thick-wristed man. Ever.

21

Sky Bluel heard the voices talking as if through a dreamy purple haze.

There were two voices. One—the tough one—was saying, "She's coming around now. You can tell by the quick intake of air."

"Looks kinda like a rodeo performer, don't she?" the other voice said. It was unctuous and familiar, although Sky couldn't quite place it.

Sky opened her eyes. At first she thought her vision was out of focus. The men were hovering directly over her, but their faces were twin pinkish blurs.

Then she realized both wore rayon stockings over their heads, which distorted their features into unrecognizability.

"Where am I?" Sky asked anxiously, pushing herself up from the cot, catching her falling granny glasses in one hand. "Is this a happening?"

"Little lady, don't you fret. You're in a safe place." The unctuous one had said that. He was shorter and wider than the other, and wore white buck shoes. It was definitely not a happening.

"If this is a safe place, why are you two dressed like Brinks bandits?" Sky demanded.

"Don't sweat it. Once you build me a neutron

bomb or two, we'll set you free to do whatever you wanna."

"Another bomb!" Sky shouted. "I just built one for Don Cooder!"

"What's she babbling about?" the unctuous voice asked the hard voice.

"That musta been what the other guy took."

"What other guy?"

"When I snatched the girl, someone else snatched this big silver thing," the hard-voiced man explained.

"Silver thing? Like a big golf ball wired up to a board?"

"It was more the size of a medicine ball."

The shorter man smacked a fist into a meaty palm, saying, "Damn! Why didn't you heist it too?"

"You said you wanted the girl."

"To build me a bomb, gumshoe! You heard her. She already had another bomb. Hell, you could've snatched the bomb and whacked her, for all I care."

"How was I to know?" the other man said in surly tones. "I never saw a neutron bomb before in my entire life."

"Can I go now?" Sky ventured.

"No!" both voices said in unison.

"What's this other guy look like?" Unctuous asked Hard Voice.

"He was filthy. Like he stepped out from a swamp."

"A Dirt Firster!"

"He might have been a street person. We were just across the street from Penn Station."

"Never mind that. We gotta get that bomb. It'll save me a whole pile of time."

"I don't like where this conversation is going,"

Sky Bluel said uneasily. "I'm getting this really freaked out feeling."

Dr. Harold W. Smith had exhausted the resources of the CURE computers. So he had fallen back on the telephone. Under the guise of being a bank-loan investigator, he had learned a great deal about Connors Swindell.

The chief source of information was Constance Payne, Swindell's secretary.

"He's a genius," she was saying. "Ouch!"

"What is the matter?" Smith asked.

"I stabbed by thumb again. They must be making these condom things thinner or something."

Smith cleared his throat, wondering if he had called at a bad time. "If we could get back to Mr. Swindell's references."

"Well, you know all about the Condome. The Western Arid Bank has the note on that. Let's see . . ."

"Does Mr. Swindell have another long-term employee I could speak to?"

"Well, there *was* Horace."

"Was?"

"Horace Feely. He was Con's—I mean Mr. Swindell's—chauffeur, but he quit suddenly, while they were in Missouri."

"Did you say chauffeur?" Smith asked suddenly.

"Yeah. He and Con go back years, which was why I thought it was so strange for him to quit like that."

"Do you know his current whereabouts?"

"If you mean Con, he just left for San Francisco."

"I meant Horace," said Smith.

"Search me, honey. He hasn't called for his check."

"Thank you."

Smith hung up and initiated a global computer search for Horace Feely. He was rewarded with a digitized photo and a rap sheet that showed Horace Feely had been a habitual criminal up until 1977, when was released from Folsum State Prison on a breaking-and-entering charge to enter the employ of a sponsor, one Connors Swindell.

It was not the record that interested Harold Smith. It was the photo. It showed a younger version of the dead body Remo had found in Missouri. The same man pictured in FBI wanted posters for having acquired the Lewisite gas that later wiped out the population of La Plomo, Missouri.

And suddenly the numbers began to tally up.

Smith picked up the phone and, calling himself Colonel Smith, got a patch-through to a military-airlift-command line.

"Remo. Smith here."

"So who's right? Chiun or me?" Remo asked. In the background, Smith heard the thundering drone of aircraft engines. After they had reported to him their failure in Manhattan, he had ordered them into the air while he confirmed his growing suspicions.

"It may be more complicated than that," Smith told him. "The Missouri body was a chauffeur, after all. He was Connors Swindell's personal chauffeur. He was not military, not Dirt First!!"

"Does that mean Dirt First!! had no part in any of this?"

"Not exactly. From eyewitness descriptions I've gleaned, it is obvious that a Dirt First!! operative took possession of the Bluel girl's latest device."

"I'm not sure I'm following this," Remo muttered.

"I did say it was complicated," Smith said.

"Uncomplicate it for me."

"Remo," Smith said urgently, "I think we have

been wrong in many of our deductions. I have been looking deeper into Connors Swindell's recent activities. There are many puzzling factors. For one thing, he is being bombarded with paternity suits."

"That wouldn't surprise me if he uses his own givaways," Remo muttered, recalling the pierced condom he had examined in La Plomo.

"These suits are all instigated by men," Smith said.

"You get what you pay for," Remo said dryly. "What else?"

"Swindell has been approaching the surviving relatives about buying up distressed La Plomo property."

"So? He's a real-estate speculator. That's his business."

"But he has already signed purchase agreements on twenty-six lots and is in active negotiation over dozens more. Remo, he is on his way to buying up the entire town, lock, stock, and barrel. And he is getting excellent bargains."

Remo frowned. "You don't mean Swindell was behind La Plomo?"

"I'm not prepared to conclude that. But it's the only scenario in which Swindell's dead chauffeur fits."

"So do we go to Palm Springs and grab Swindell," Remo asked, "or San Francisco and grab the neutron bomb from what's left of Dirt First?"

Smith was silent. The picture was still very confused. He would have to make an imperfect decision, and they were always dangerous.

"According to his secretary, Swindell left for San Francisco just hours ago," Smith said at last. "It's possible he's in cahoots with Dirt First!!—bizarre as that may sound. Go there."

"It sounds ridiculous," Remo growled, "but it's all we have."

* * *

In the rear of the C-130 transport, Remo hung up the phone.

"We're going to San Francisco," he told the Master of Sinanju, watching for a reaction.

Chiun nodded. The tightly etched wrinkles of his face faded with relief. His ivory countenance had been the bloodless hue of bone. Now it suffused with color again.

"Great is my joy upon hearing your words," said the Master of Sinanju. "I will so inform the pilot."

"Be my guest," Remo said, staring at Chiun's retreating figure. The Master of Sinanju had actually been terrified of returning to Palm Springs. Well, Remo thought, that won't happen now. And whatever happened, Remo would be there to protect his teacher.

Barry Kranish was packing when the downstairs buzzer intruded. He let it buzz. If it was trouble, why let it in? If it wasn't, there was no one Barry Kranish cared to see on his last night in San Francisco. He threw his last bottle of jagua juice into the suitcase and closed it tight.

The buzzing stopped. Kranish lugged two overstuffed suitcases downstairs to the lobby, where an addled woodsy owl hung upside down in its cage and Venezuelan bull roaches ranged freely. Just as it should be.

The two men with the stockings over their heads were not. One held a revolver in his fist. It was pointed at Barry.

"Let's go for a ride," the gunman said in a smoky Humphrey Bogart voice.

"Where?"

"To wherever you put that neutron bomb." This

came from the other one. He sounded like Joe Isuzu on meds.

"I'll never tell!" Kranish spat, letting the suitcases fall. "You can do anything you want. Even wild *candiru* couldn't suck it out of me!"

"I can fix that attitude," the gunman said. "I do it all the—"

Noticing a cockroach scuttling by his feet, he carelessly lifted a brogan to crush out its tiny life.

"No!" Barry Kranish said, dropping to his knees. "That's a bull cockroach. Please don't harm it. I'll tell you anything!"

If it were possible for a man wearing a stocking mask to register an incredulous expression, this one did. But he recovered from his surprise fast enough to spit out, "Then talk quick or the bug gets it."

"Yeah," the other added. "Then we'll do the owl."

"Not the owl!" Kranish cried. His pain woke the threatened bird. Its wings thrashed in panic. "Palm Springs! It's down in Palm Springs!"

"Why there?" The owl-endangerer put that question forward.

"It's a blot on the perfect sanctity of the delicate desert."

"Palm Springs? A blot?"

"It should be stamped out forever so the sands can blow freely," Barry Kranish said passionately. "So the cactus can spread its needles without fear. So the scorpion may dance in the dust devils, as it did before the white man came despoiling."

"Okay, here's the old sixty-four-thousand-dollar question," asked the man with the Joe Isuzu voice. "Where is the bomb?"

"I hid it in a hotel room."

"Why there?"

"So no one would bother it until it detonates.

Actually, I really wanted to nuke that Condome, but I couldn't get a rental car. The agency was closed because of an unexpected death."

"Christ! You armed it?" This from the gunman.

"It's the only way to get the message of Dirt First!! to the world. Over the next five days, media outlets all over America will begin receiving Dirt First!! faxes. If Palm Springs is not razed and restored in its natural barren splendor, then the device will detonate and only the ecologically insensitive will perish."

"The nuke won't go up for five days?" asked the man with the oily salesman's voice.

"That's right."

"Okay, that gives us plenty of time to get to it." The gunman waggled his revolver in the direction of the open front door. "Let's take a little trip."

Obligingly the owl-threatener led the way. Kranish followed. The masked gunman fell in behind him.

On the way out, Kranish heard a tiny crunch. He winced, hoping the insensitive gunman hadn't harmed one of nature's most perfect creatures. It would be one less insect brain to preserve the memory of selfless Barry Kranish in the coming post-human epoch.

Remo and Chiun arrived less than an hour later to find the front door to Dirt First!! headquarters ajar.

"Oh-oh," Remo said, motioning for the Master of Sinanju to hang back. "Looks like the barn door's open. Better let me go first."

"Over my dead body," spat the Master of Sinanju, pushing past Remo. He strode into the reception room, shaking his tiny fists and shouting at the top of his mighty lungs.

"Enemies of America, come show your villainous faces!" he cried. "The Master of Sinanju, wise in years, but still sound of limb despite his advancing years, challenges you!"

Remo rolled his eyes. "Little Father, you have nothing to prove to—"

Chiun lifted a hand for silence. He cocked one ear, then the other. "I detect no sounds. This domicile is vacant. Can your ears tell you the same story, O callow youth?"

"I'll take your word for it." Remo noticed two suitcases balanced on the winding staircase. He opened them, finding a bottle of familiar yellow-brown juice. "Looks like Kranish was about to split," he said, "and something interrupted him. Maybe the good guys, maybe the bad. Either way, it's a dead end. Come on, let's look for the bomb. Not that we'll find it."

They didn't find the bomb. But in a wastebasket next to an antique Remington typewriter, Remo dug out a crumpled ball of papers. Written on Dirt First!! stationery, they were discarded drafts of a communiqué warning of the imminent destruction of Palm Springs, California.

The Master of Sinanju drifted in while Remo was reading these drafts.

"You have found something?" he asked.

"No," Remo said hastily, dropping the papers into the basket. "Just old mash notes from the Sierra Club. Looks like he abandoned ship for sure."

"Perhaps Emperor Smith may guide us," Chiun suggested.

"Good idea," Remo said quickly. "Let's find a phone."

There was one in the next room. Remo had to blow dust off the receiver before he dared pick it up. He got Smith on the first ring.

"Smitty?" he said, turning around to see if Chiun

was in earshot. To his surprise, the Master of Sinanju had drifted to another room. Great, Remo thought. "Listen up, Smitty," Remo said, *sotto voce*. "Kranish is gone. There's no sign of Swindell. But the neutron bomb's been planted in a Palm Springs hotel. The Thousand Palms. It's set to blow in five days."

"Remo, are you sure of this?" Smith demanded.

"I just read the rough drafts. The idiot even gave the room number in the first draft. He must be pretty confident that no one can dismantle the device."

"No one except Sky Bluel, wherever she is. Remo, go to Palm Springs immediately."

"Chiun isn't going to like this," Remo warned.

"Then leave him behind. The fact that the device is in Palm Springs points back to Connors Swindell."

"I'll be in touch," Remo said, hanging up.

Remo found the Master of Sinanju down in the reception area, feeding live cockroaches to the fish.

"I talked to Smith," Remo began. "He says we should split up. You stay here and wait for Kranish or somebody to show. I'll grab Swindell and wring the truth out of him."

Chiun dropped a frightened cockroach into a tank and watched the fish converge on it. He kept his back to Remo.

"Do not lie to me, Remo Williams," he said severely. "I know you too well after all these years."

"Okay, you got me," Remo admitted. "The bomb is in Palm Springs. It's armed, but we have five days to disarm it. Plenty of time. Since you have a phobia about going back there, why don't I handle it?"

Chiun turned, hazel eyes narrowing. "No," he said.

"Look, what's the big deal? It's Vimu and Songjong all over again, isn't it? Okay, I'm Songjong. I'm telling you, Vimu, to stay here and guard the gold while I go into the Egyptian desert to handle the wicked pretender."

"He was a princeling, not a pretender."

"Whatever. The legend fits. Admit it. I should go and you should stay. It's a piece-of-cake gig for both of us."

Chiun's eyes squeezed down to sightless slits.

"You believe because I am old, I have grown afraid," he intoned.

"It's not that. Heck, I didn't know you were pushing a hundred until you told me. It's just that you have this thing about Palm Springs. Dealing with a nuke is tricky enough. I don't want to have to watch you too."

"I am no child who needs watching!" Chiun exploded. "I am the Reigning Master of Sinanju and I am not afraid to go into the desert, no matter what perils await."

Remo threw up his hands in surrender.

"Okay, okay! You win. Let's go. But if we miss a solid lead because of you, you get to break the bad news to Smith."

"I do not think it will be me breaking bad news to Emperor Smith," Chiun said as they walked from the rundown San Francisco Victorian. "But I go without fear, for I am unafraid. As always."

22

Because they had military-airlift-command helicopters at their disposal, Remo and Chiun reached the Palm Springs Municipal Airport within an hour. A cab took them to the Thousand Palms Hotel, a palatial Spanish-Moorish monstrosity of stucco and red-tile roofs sprawling on the edge of the desert.

From the lobby they called Room 334 on a house phone.

"It's just ringing," Remo told the Master of Sinanju. "I don't think anyone's up there."

Chiun nodded. He looked about the lobby, as if preoccupied.

They took the elevator and followed a long curved corridor to Room 334. The lock was the key type. Remo simply put his fist to the keyhole, drew back, and punched hard once.

The door jumped inward on its hinges, the tongue of the lock having gouged out a notch in the inner doorjamb.

Before Remo could stop him, the Master of Sinanju leapt into the room. He whirled twice, in different directions, as if to deal with unseen attackers.

Then, lowering his crooked nails in disappointment, he faced Remo.

"This den of evil appears to be empty," he admitted.

"No kidding," Remo said dryly, closing the door behind him. He went around the room, checking in the bathroom and under the bed. Chiun poked about the dresser drawers, dropping the Gideon Bible into the wastebasket.

"Found it!" Remo said, flinging open a long clothes closet.

The Master of Sinanju drew up alongside him.

The neutron device gleamed like a model radome equipped with convenient carrying handles.

"I do not hear ticking," Chiun noted.

"These things don't tick," Remo said, dropping to his knees. He tested the stainless-steel handles on the shaped charges. They were locked up tight. He dismissed pulling them out by force. No telling what might result.

His eyes went to a digital counter welded to the breadboard electronics.

The digital numbers were bright red: 01:21:44.

"Looks like the countdown is definitely under way," Remo said.

"Did you not say there remained five days until this contraption explodes?" Chiun asked.

"That's what Kranish's dippy drafts said. Five days."

"If I read this correctly, this neutral device is but an hour from booming."

Remo blinked. He peered closer. "You must be mistaken, Little Father. It's five days. See the last digits, 44? That probably means 4.4 days or something like that."

But even as Remo spoke, the last two digits became 43. Then 42. Then 41.

"What do you say now?" Chiun asked.

"I think we could use a third opinion," Remo said worriedly.

As she was shoved into the back of the car, Sky Bluel collided with the man sitting in back. His eyes were too round.

"Who's he?" she asked as the two stocking-masked men got in front. The car started off. She didn't know where she was. The familiar California date palms offered no comfort. She bit her lower lip.

"That," the driver with the smoky Humphrey Bogart voice said, "is the jerk who heisted your neutron bomb."

"No way!" Sky said. "That guy needed a bath."

"Take my word for it, girlie."

"Girlie! When were you born, back in the fifties?"

"As a matter of fact—"

The other man cut in. "I hope you know how to disarm that bomb, little lady."

"Sure, I got the key right here around . . ." Sky's mouth froze in a perfect O.

"What's that?"

"Nothing," Sky Bluel said in a weak voice, feeling the absence of a key around her throat.

"I thought you said something about a key."

"Oh, right. I don't suppose you guys found my luggage key? I had it around my neck."

"Don't sweat it. Your luggage is safe in New York."

Sky Bluel swallowed. "So's the key. Probably."

They parked in a corner of the Thousand Palms Hotel lot, and Sky Bluel was pulled out of the back, along with the other captive, who hadn't spoken a solitary word during the short ride.

"Just walk ahead of us and don't turn back." A revolver nudging her ribs prodded Sky along.

They slipped in the kitchen entrance and up a flight of steps to the third floor and Room 334. While the man with the revolver held them at bay, the other man reached for the doorknob with one hand and into his coat pocket with the other.

He pulled out a hotel key and said, "This key is the only one that counts." His broad grin shone through the sheer rayon like a polished bone.

Then the doorknob was abruptly yanked inward, taking him and his smile with it. The look on his thick flattened face as he disappeared was comical.

Remo Williams released the swinging door and grabbed Connors Swindell by the back of the neck. His nails zipped up the back of Swindell's head, causing the stocking mask to peel off and drop to the floor.

"We meet again," Remo said.

With a deft twist of his wrist, he sent Swindell bouncing on the bed. The Master of Sinanju's hand slapped him once into submission.

"Watch him, Chiun," Remo said. "I'll get the others."

There were three of them, Remo discovered. Sky Bluel, Barry Kranish, and a third guy he didn't recognize, and not due to his stocking mask. His body shape was unfamiliar. This man was holding a revolver on the other two. He shifted the weapon toward Remo.

As if a revolver were no more menacing than a rolled-up newspaper, Remo pointed to the revolver with one finger.

"You don't know it, pal, but you're outgunned."

Before the gunman could complete his defiant sneer, Remo's right arm snapped forward, jamming the rigid forefinger into the gun barrel. He crooked his finger. The gun barrel broke off.

Grinning, Remo lifted the barrel, still wrapped around his finger, under the gunman's nose. The latter's eyes crossed trying to keep it in focus.

"It's fast-answer time," Remo suggested brightly.

"I . . . I'm just an employee," the gunman blurted out. "I work for Mr. Swindell. That's all! I got nothing to do with the big picture."

"Are you sure?" Remo asked politely.

"Positive. I'm a private dick. Just a cog in the machine."

"The machine," Remo said, returning the gun barrel through the surprisingly fragile bone of Calvin Taggert's forehead, "just broke down.

"Won't you step into my office?" Remo asked the others as the gunman got down on the rug and shook the life out of his body.

Sky Bluel all but jumped into the hotel room. Barry Kranish needed a push, which suited Remo just fine. He used his foot.

"Okay, people," Remo sang out, closing the door behind him. "It's show-and-tell time." He pushed the closet door open, revealing the silent neutron bomb with its screaming red digital display. "There, that's the show. Now, let's hear the tell." Remo's deadly finger waved back and forth among the three captives. "Starting with . . . " The finger stopped, pointing at Connors Swindell, sprawled on the bed, mopping his forehead. "You!"

"I'm innocent," Swindell said hastily.

"Are you sure?" Remo asked.

"Swear to God I am."

Connors Swindell sat up. He grinned the grin that had moved a million units during the last two decades. It always made people feel good.

And while his accusers were basking in his feel-good smile, Connors Swindell slipped his sopping handkerchief to his mouth and nose and went for his Waterman.

He got it out lickety-split. Thumbing the cap off, he pointed it at the skinny guy and the old Oriental. He pressed the ink trigger.

Nothing happened.

"Where's the gas?" he asked, dumbfounded.

"Coming out you at both ends," Remo Williams said, snatching up the pen. He showed the yellow fluid in the ink reservoir to Chiun. "What do you think, Chiun?"

The Master of Sinanju looked from the Waterman to Swindell's profusely sweating face. "I think my judgment is vindicated. I knew he was an impostor from the first. Let this be a lesson to you, Remo."

"I don't get it," Swindell muttered thickly.

Remo showed him the hollow end of the pen. Swindell tried to draw back, but Remo took him by the hair and put his nose to the pen tip.

"It was simple," he said. "You uncapped the pen. Then you pressed the trigger."

"I know that. I was there."

"In between, I squeezed the needle flat. No bad stuff can come out now."

"That's flat impossible!" Swindell complained. "No one's that quick."

"Sue me," Remo said, shoving him flat on his back.

The Master of Sinanju interrupted. "Should we not dispose of this neutral device before we attend to these criminals?" he asked Remo.

"What's the rush?" Remo said. "We have five days before it goes off."

Sky Bluel jumped. "Five days?"

"Yeah, it's set for five days," Remo said. "Right, Kranish?"

Looking hollow-eyed, Barry Kranish spoke for the first time. "I have nothing to say until someone reads me my rights," he said thickly.

"Five days," Sky Bluel repeated. "The timer doesn't have a five-day setting."

"What?" Kranish said. "I pressed five."

"How long ago?" Sky Bluel asked, her voice climbing in horror.

"I don't know. Hours ago." Kranish's voice was distracted.

"Let me see," Sky said, rushing to the device. She had to examine it only a second or two.

"Evacuate!" she shrieked. "We have to evacuate! It's going off in twenty minutes!"

"What!" Kranish said. He rushed for the door. Remo tripped him, holding him down on the rug with a foot to the back of the lawyer's neck. Kranish struggled like a pinned scorpion.

"Can you disarm it?" Remo asked Sky Bluel.

"Not the mechanism," Sky said in a miserable voice. "The only chance is to remove the plastique charges."

"Is there enough time?"

"There is if I had the key," Sky moaned. "Which I don't."

"Why the hell not?" Remo shouted.

"Yeah, why the hell not?" Kranish echoed. Remo shut him up with a sudden pressure to his spinal column.

"I think it got lost when the other guy tried to kidnap me."

"Any other way of disarming it?"

"I could try, but there may not be enough time. And if it goes off, everybody for miles around will be killed."

Remo and Chiun exchanged glances. Remo's was anxious. The Master of Sinanju's face registered a cold acceptance of fate.

"What if we drive it out into the desert?" Remo asked Sky.

"That might save the town, but not us."

"I vote we leave it and head for the hills," Swindell piped up. Chiun silenced him with a smack from the flat of his hand.

Remo turned to Sky. "Are you game to defuse it with me?"

Sky Bluel swallowed. "It's my responsibility," she said simply.

"Chiun. We don't need you on this one."

Chiun lifted his bearded chin stubbornly. "I am coming."

"Look, I've got no time to argue with you," Remo said tensely. "We're going back out there. You stay with Swindell."

"Good idea," Connors Swindell said with relief.

Chiun reached out and lifted Connors Swindell off the bed. "No," he intoned. "Those who made this mess must be prepared to clean it up or suffer the consequences."

"All right, let's go," Remo said savagely. "There isn't time to argue." He gathered up the bomb, carrying it down in the elevator and to the waiting car.

Remo drove.

"Is there any other road into the desert that doesn't take us by the Condome?" Remo asked Swindell.

"No, that's the only one. You can drop me off if you want."

"No chance," Remo growled, flooring the gas.

He put Palm Springs behind him. In the back seat, Sky Bluel, Barry Kranish, and Connors Swindell sat, the neutron bomb distributed among their laps. Remo thought that would give them extra motivation.

"Maybe if I unscrew the electronics," Sky was saying. "Anyone have a screwdriver?"

No one did. "How about a dime?" Swindell asked, plumbing his pockets for change.

Sky used the dime. She got one screw loose. "That's one." She did not sound encouraged.

"What's the timer say?" Remo asked.

"It says sixteen minutes and three seconds," Sky said. "I'm not sure I'm going to get this done in time."

"Let's all bail out here," Swindell suggested. "Dump the thing in the sand and skedaddle back to town. What say?"

"Can we make it?" Remo asked Sky.

"We might, but Palm Springs is still in the kill zone. Oh, why did I build this thing?"

"Because you're stupid," Remo said, pushing the gas pedal into the floorboards.

"Remo," Chiun said solemnly.

"What?"

"I see only once chance for any of us."

"I'm listening."

"One of us must carry the device into the desert, alone. While the other drives in the opposite direction to safety."

"Ridiculous," Sky snapped. "You'd have to run faster than a car to do that!"

"I'll do it," Remo offered.

"No," Chiun said in a resigned tone. "You are the future of Sinanju, Remo. I am only its past. The line must continue. So I must do this."

Remo braked. "Cut the martyr act, Chiun. It's old. You're good, sure, but you're not as fast as me. I'm younger, stronger, and I can get further faster. So stuff your silly Korean pride and face reality. I'm the only one for this job, and we both know it."

Stung, the Master of Sinanju said nothing for several long moments.

"So, that is how you feel about me," he said softly.

"Facts are facts," Remo said impatiently, jumping from the car. Opening the passenger door, he reached in for the neutron device.

He wasn't caught entirely unawares. Remo did sense the minuscule pressure of Chiun's hand pushing air ahead of it as it struck the base of his skull and turned his world black.

The Master of Sinanju pushed Remo into the back with one hand. The other pulled Sky Bluel from the same seat.

"You will drive," he told her. "And drive swiftly. For my son must live."

"This is crazy," Sky said. "There must be another way."

"There was. But it died when you built this device. Go."

Chin trembling, Sky Bluel got behind the wheel. "Good luck," she said weakly.

The car made a skittering circle in the road and headed back to town, leaving the Master of Sinanju holding the neutron bomb in his spindly arms.

Chiun looked down at the foreign instrument. His hazel eyes glanced at the digital timer. It now read 00:05:57. Then 00:05:56.

Lifting his eyes, he sought the place where the desert Condome had been. He drew in an energizing breath.

In that direction, Chiun began running. His sandals whetted the road. He picked up speed, and his purple kimono began to stream behind him with the gathering force of his momentum.

As he ran, Chiun beseeched his ancestors to prepare a seat of honor for the last pure-blooded Master of Sinanju.

Remo woke up suddenly. He bolted up in the seat, realized where he was, and looked around the careening car.

"Where's Chiun?" he demanded savagely.

Sky bit her lip. "Back there."

Remo looked back.

"How long?" he croaked.

"Any minute now," Sky Bluel whispered, tears rolling down her face.

Remo flung open the car door, mentally calculating the speed of the car versus the counterforce he would have to apply if he was to alight in one piece.

One foot went out. It scraped the road like sandpaper.

Then Remo's eyes widened into dark explosions of fear.

The noise was not loud. Its muffled quality made it all the more heart-stopping. It was like something deep and important erupting in the bowels of the earth.

Remo looked back. They all looked back, except Sky, who was sobbing uncontrollably as her eyes shifted between the road ahead and the sight in the rearview mirror.

It was not a mushroom cloud. Not in the classic sense. It was more of a violent upflinging of sand and smoke. A boiling fist spewed up amid the climbing sand like ball lightning and then spent itself like a flash paper dragon.

"Are we far enough from it?" Remo demanded, sick-eyed.

"I think so," Sky said chokingly.

The shock wave was short and violent and hot. It sent the car skidding sideways into the sand. It stopped, rear wheels spinning uselessly. Remo got out. He looked back at the smoky cloud, his eyes stricken.

Sky clung to his side. The others emerged too. But only to crawl under the car, where they thought it was safe.

"I don't see him," Remo said thickly. "Do you?"

Sky shook her head so hard hot tears splashed on Remo's arms. "No way he could have escaped that," she sobbed. "No way."

Remo turned on Sky Bluel. "I don't believe you!" He grabbed her by the arms, shaking her. "Tell me the truth!"

"Look. I don't know how he was able to run with that thing in the first place, but for him to escape the neutron bombardment, he'd have had to be outside the kill zone. On this side. And I don't see him. Anywhere."

Remo's eyes scoured the surrounding terrain. There was no sign of Chiun on the undulant dunes.

"I'm going in," Remo said.

In desperation Sky grabbed his shirt. "You'll be killed. We should be getting further away. The neutrons are coming this way. You can't see them or feel them, but they'll slam into your cells like microscopic bullets. Slow, agonizing death."

Remo tore free. "You go if you want to," he spat. He started off into the desert.

Remo ran at a steady clip, sticking to the road until it changed direction away from the smoky cloud on the horizon.

"Come on, Chiun," he whispered. "Show your face. I know you're out there. Come on."

Remo covered a good quarter-mile without spotting any life. Then he began to feel something in the air.

It was like a little pinprick on his bare right arm. Just a pinprick, but it stung like a red-hot needle. Remo pressed on. Another pinprick struck his chest. And another.

He had felt a similar sensation before. Once, while standing too close to a leaky microwave oven.

Remo knew then he was running into the leading edge of neutron bombardment, which his finely tuned body met and absorbed. It was like running into an acid spray. He knew the spray would swell to a deadly storm at any moment.

"Chiun!" Remo cried, shifting direction. He tried running in a widening circle, keeping just outside and ahead of the spreading radiation field.

No answer came from the kill zone.

Then, because he knew to go on was to die, Remo Williams abruptly reversed direction.

He fought to hold down the hot choking lump that struggled to climb out of his throat.

Remo caught up with the car as it approached the Palm Springs city limits. Running alongside, he signaled Sky to pull over.

Not quite believing her eyes, Sky did.

"Are you all right?" she asked.

Remo said nothing. He went to the rear door and pulled it off its hinges. That got the attention of the passengers in back.

Connors Swindell fought to get away from the hand that reached in for his throat.

"This is all your fault, isn't it?" Remo raged, yanking him to his feet.

Swindell pointed at Barry Kranish, cowering in the car, saying, "No, it's his fault. You, tell him."

Remo reached in for Barry Kranish. He pulled him out by his microwaved hair.

"If he'd left the poor scorpions alone," Kranish snapped, "none of this would have happened."

"No more lies!" Remo shouted. "No more bull-shit! What was this all about?"

Connors Swindell and Barry Kranish looked into the deadly dark eyes of Remo Williams and decided to tell the truth. Unfortunately, they tried to tell it simultaneously.

Remo shook them in his strong hands.

"In one word, what was this all about?" he repeated.

"Property," said Connors Swindell.

"The environment," said Barry Kranish.

Remo looked at them coldly for a long time.

"The most important person in my life just died because of you. Tell me he died for something more than a real-estate scam and saving the weasels."

"Look," Swindell said, grinning sickly, "I can see that you're hurtin'. But you gotta put this into perspective. He was old, an empty nester. If they don't go when they get ripe, property would never change hands. And then where would the world be?"

Remo Williams looked at Connors Swindell's sweating face as if not believing the evidence of his ears.

"You know what you are?" he asked evenly.

"Under arrest?" Swindell ventured weakly.

"No, landfill," Remo replied, giving Connors Swindell's neck a sudden squeeze. His head shot up twenty feet in the air. It landed at the base of a palm like a ripe coconut. Remo threw the body on top with a savagely careless fling.

Then he turned his attention to Barry Kranish.

"You love trees?" he asked in a too-even tone.

"I love life even more," Kranish said, sick-voiced.

"Fine, let's feed a few trees."

"I didn't bring any tree food."

"You *are* the tree food," Remo explained.

Remo escorted Barry Kranish behind a stately date palm and carefully converted him into mulch. When he returned a moment later, he was washing the blood off his hands with sand.

Sky Bluel didn't stick around to find out what had happened to the late Barry Kranish. She jumped behind the wheel and drove into town without a backward glance.

Remo let her go. She wasn't important anymore.

He turned to face the desert. The smoke cloud now hung low against the horizon. A hot wind tore at it like fingers plucking at an old rag.

Remo sat down on the edge of the road and with sunken eyes watched the too-hot wind tear the clouds to shreds and carry the faint fragments away.

He refused to move until the sun came up to turn its accusing red eye on him.

23

Three months later, the high corn was tasseling outside of La Plomo, Missouri.

Heirs had been arriving all summer in a steady stream to reclaim the homes of their dead relatives. Farms were taken over. Plans were made to plow under the Lewisite-tainted crops. It was a sad event. But next year there would be another, better crop.

La Plomo was coming back to life.

By this time the sun had entered Leo, and the Federal Emergency Management Agency had declared a blasted area of desert four miles outside of Palm Springs, California, to be radiation-free. FEMA also promised to release a two-million-dollar study by Christmas explaining how a nuclear accident had occurred in an area where nuclear tests were not authorized.

The official report would be a tissue of vague lies cloaked under the umbrella of national security, but only a handful of people knew that, including one Sky Bluel, who had dyed her hair green and flown off to finish her education in Paris.

On the day after the desert had been declared free of radiation, wearing a black T-shirt and matching chinos, Remo Williams walked out into the shifting sands.

His face was set and devoid of readable emotion as he reached the flat blob of fused glass that marked the core blast area. It was less than a dozen feet in diameter. Black in the center, shading to bubble-pocked brown, the ragged outer edges were clear and streaked with tadpolelike air pockets. The tadpoles seemed frozen in the act of fleeing the blast.

Remo stepped onto the fused sand. He had left no footprints arriving, and the glass barely gave under his weight.

He walked to the exact center, an upthrust crater of obsidian shards, where critical mass had fused the fine sand. The ground was littered with discarded Styrofoam coffee cups and cigarette butts left by FEMA crisis managers.

Remo's eyes tuned out these artifacts. He was scanning for a single color. Royal purple—the color of the kimono Chiun had last worn. All he wanted was a tiny bit of purple silk. Something—anything—to take back to Sinanju for burial.

He had accepted the Master of Sinanju's death weeks ago. What he couldn't accept was the absence of a body. He understood that Chiun must have been holding the neutron bomb when it went critical. He understood how the blast could have obliterated an ordinary human being.

But not Chiun. Not the Master of Sinanju. Something would have survived. Something had to have survived.

But nothing had. Nothing tangible.

Remo walked east. The Plexiglas dome of Connors Swindell's last grandiose scheme, the Condome, had been dismantled. All that remained was a huge plug of concrete poured to seal off the buried tower for all time. The sand had already drifted over the ugly gray cap. In a few generations it would be something for archaeologists to ponder. Now it was only a monument to one greedy man's folly.

Remo walked the desert half the night. The moon rose and its clear silver light provided enough illumination for his Sinanju-trained eyes to see by.

He found no evidence to prove that here in this desert—so remote that the scrolls of Sinanju did not record its name—on the threshold of the venerated age, the greatest Master of Sinanju, Chiun the Great, had sacrificed himself so that the line could continue in the body of an unworthy white man.

Standing alone in the desert, Remo felt an emotion sweep over him. It was one he had not experienced in a very long time. He felt inadequate.

Remo lifted his voice to the morning star, which had just appeared low in the east.

"Oh, Little Father," he said sorrowfully, "where are you now? I feel lost without you. I'm not ready for this."

He felt a presence suddenly. Behind him. Remo whirled.

"Chiun!"

Standing there, hands tucked into the folds of a simple kimono, stood the Master of Sinanju, his head bowed. He was a dim figure, his kimono two shades darker than purple, his face pale like a birchwood bust decorated with cotton streamers for hair and beard.

Chiun's half-shadowed mouth moved as if in prayer, but no sounds were reaching Remo's ears.

"Little Father, is that really you?" Remo asked. But his ears told him it was not. Not really. He detected no biological sounds. He sensed the presence before him as a cold force, but it was not living. Not anymore.

Chiun lifted his eyes. They were a deeper gray than hazel, and infinitely sad.

One claw of a hand came out of its sleeve. It pointed toward Remo, slanting downward.

Remo looked down at his feet. He frowned.

"What about my shoes?"

The hand recoiled and pointed again, like an accusing specter.

"I don't understand," Remo said, his voice anxious. "What are you trying to tell me?"

The claw of a hand shifted. The Master of Sinanju pointed to the ground at his own feet. His eyes were imploring.

A gleam came into Remo's dark eyes. Remo nodded. "I get it. I'm head of the House of Sinanju now. From this day on, I walk in your sandals."

Remo bowed from the waist, saying, "I understand. I will honor you by carrying on the work. Farewell, Little Father."

When Remo straightened, he beheld the Master of Sinanju lift his face and hands to the stars in a gesture of despair. His mouth made a silent, anguished shape.

Then, like a star dying, he faded from sight.

And Remo Williams, feeling the immense burden of five thousand years of responsibility, sank to his knees in the sand and wept without shame.